DEATH SPIRAL

DEATH SPIRAL

•

Clyde Linsley

AVALON BOOKS
NEW YORK

PRINTED IN THE UNITED STATES OF AMERICA
ON ACID-FREE PAPER
BY HADDON CRAFTSMEN, BLOOMSBURG, PENNSYLVANIA

To Nancy, with love.

Prologue

The gun worried me the most.

He had one, and I didn't. That fact shifted the balance of power in his direction.

Of course, he didn't know I was still alive. That gave me the advantage of surprise. Somehow, I didn't think that would be enough.

The parking lot was lit by two mercury-vapor lamps, one at each end, which caused the snow to take on a greenish cast. He would be coming from the woods, just beyond the farthest lamppost. He would be lit briefly in that pool of light and then he would be past it, on his way to his car. That would be my best chance of evening the odds, when I would be in darkness and he would be in the light.

Man, it was cold.

Would he have the gun out? Probably not. He wouldn't be expecting trouble at this stage. And he was no expert with it, either. Still, he was good enough. He had used it twice that I knew of—and once that I had seen—and it had killed its intended victims with remarkable efficiency. Of course, in both instances he was shooting at point-blank range. At a greater distance he would probably be less accurate.

But he hadn't hesitated to kill. He'd planned the most recent murder for a long time and had taken steps to ensure success, and when the time came he hadn't been troubled by pangs of conscience.

And there had been at least one more murder, years ago, and who knew how many between? Whatever else he might have been, he wasn't afraid to act.

So the trick would be to disarm him before he got within point-blank range. But to do that I would need some sort of weapon of my own.

What could it be? A tree limb? I didn't see any lying on the ground.

Or would he come at all? Maybe I had made an inaccurate assumption about his plans. Maybe he had another car waiting somewhere else, and I was waiting here in vain. It wouldn't have been the first time I had misjudged this case. While I was shivering here in the snow, he could be on his way to Baltimore.

But I didn't think so. I thought I knew him well enough by now. In another fifteen minutes or so he would come out of the woods on a dead run, and I would be the last line of defense.

So here I was, shivering behind a snowbank in a deserted parking lot in Rock Creek Park, waiting for a murderer to come running out of the woods. A murderer who was still carrying the murder weapon.

And what did I have to fight him with?

I looked around me.

Snow. Nothing but snow.

This was no way to spend a Saturday night.

Chapter One

It hadn't seemed such a big deal in the beginning. In fact, it hadn't seemed like a case at all.

It had begun the previous Monday afternoon, when I stepped into an ice rink in upper Northwest Washington. A knot of spectators stood off to one side of the rink. A stocky man in an olive V-neck sweater with a T-shirt showing underneath detached himself from the group and lumbered in my direction. He had precisely 2.3 chins, which is the number normally allotted to an entire American household. We're big on statistics in Washington, D.C.

"Mr. McFarlin?" He had a sandpaper voice.

"That's right."

"I'm Jack Dumas," he said, extending a paw. "I'm the rink manager."

"You're the one who called me."

"That's right. We've been waiting for you over here. Won't you join us?"

"Lead the way," I said.

He started to move off. I could see him looking me over, the way you might inspect a questionable used car. He resisted the impulse to kick my tires.

"You're very young," he said. It wasn't quite an

accusation, more like a hypothesis that he expected me to disprove.

"Shall I come back tomorrow? I'll be older then."

He sighed, just once. "Come with me," he said.

Since Dumas was with me, the party now consisted of two women, one of them fortyish, the other perhaps ten years younger. They began moving in our direction, meeting us halfway.

"Where's the girl I'm supposed to keep an eye on?" I asked.

"She isn't here right now," Dumas said. "Her mother wanted to meet you first."

The older woman reached us and offered her hand. She was a striking woman, with hair that was nearly black, deep dimples, high cheekbones, and blue eyes that teetered on the edge of violet, the way Elizabeth Taylor's eyes are supposed to do.

"I'm Irene Liston, Mr. McFarlin," she said. She had a smile to go with her face, warm and cool at the same time. "Thank you for coming all the way out here. I'm afraid I wouldn't have been comfortable discussing this in your office."

"I don't mind," I said. "I'm not comfortable in my office, either."

"I don't know how much Jack told you on the phone."

"Only that your daughter was in danger."

She made a face. "That may be putting it a bit . . . strongly. There have been, well, threats I suppose. I don't know whether to take them seriously."

"Tell me about them."

"I had a phone call yesterday morning," she said.

"I was getting ready to leave for the office when the phone rang. I answered it and a voice said, 'Debbie Liston will die.' "

"Then what?"

"He hung up," she said. "I had a feeling that he perhaps had intended to say more but had forgotten the words."

"You mean he had memorized a speech?"

"No, I don't believe so. It's as if he wanted to get something off his chest and then froze when he had the opportunity."

"You say 'he.' It was a man's voice, I gather."

"Well, a male voice, anyway. Fairly young, I think, and high pitched."

"Could it have been a prank?" I asked. "Some kid in the neighborhood?"

"That was my first reaction," she said. "But we live in an older neighborhood, and there are not many young persons nearby. And then there was a second call this morning. It came at about the same time as yesterday, and it was the same voice. This time, he said, 'Debbie Liston will die if she doesn't stop skating.' *Then* he hung up."

"It still sounds a little like a prank to me," I said.

"And then Jane told me she saw a strange man loitering outside my house yesterday afternoon."

"Who's Jane?" I asked.

The other woman had joined us by now. Mrs. Liston said, "This is Jane Borman, Debbie's skating coach."

Jane Borman had short, raw-umber hair and lines etched lightly at the corner of her eyes. It was not a perfect face, especially when compared to Irene Liston's, but it was a likeable face.

"Tell me about the man you saw," I said.

"I didn't see him well," she said. "He was parked in front of Irene's house yesterday, and he kept staring at it."

"Any distinguishing features?"

"I couldn't see his face," she said. "He was in his car, and I saw him through the windshield. I wouldn't recognize him."

"How did you know he was staring at the house?"

"He had binoculars. I'd call that staring."

"So would I," I said. "What time was this?"

"About three," she said. "I'd come over to discuss Debbie and Jerry's program. Debbie was up in her room, and I was waiting for her downstairs. I happened to wander over to the window and look out, and there he was."

"What kind of car?"

"A small car, yellow."

"License number?"

"I didn't think to look," she said. "I *did* notice a dent in the left front fender, and there were some of those foam rubber dice hanging from the rearview mirror. Blue."

"How long was the car there?"

"I don't know," she said. "I was there for about an hour, and it was gone when I left."

"How about it?" Dumas said to me. "Will you take the job?"

"I don't think there *is* a job," I said. "It sounds to

me like someone playing some sort of amateurish prank."

Irene Liston started to protest, but Dumas shook her off, and she clamped her lips shut and turned away. Jane Borman said to her, "It's all right, Irene. There are other investigators."

Dumas walked away from the group and stood near the glass barrier that surrounded the ice. He beckoned to me with his index finger. I crossed over and stood beside him.

"Why not?"

"Why won't I take the job? Because I'd be wasting your money."

"It's my money. Let me waste it. You got so much business you can afford to turn down paying clients?"

He had a point. In Washington, if you only take the jobs that are necessary, you could wait a long time between paychecks. You don't see the government refusing to do a job just because the job doesn't need doing.

"Let me tell you about this," Dumas said. "See that kid out there?" He pointed to a girl tracing solitary figures on the otherwise empty ice.

"I noticed her when I came in."

"Cute kid, huh? Name's Mary. She's here maybe twenty hours a week, all told. Not a bad skater, either. Almost made the cut at the junior regionals last year. If she had, she'd have gone on to the sectional championships and then the nationals. And she might make it someday. But you know what?"

"What?"

"The best day of her career, she won't be one-tenth

the skater Debbie Liston is going to be. And she knows it."

"So what's your point?"

"My point is, you want a reason why somebody wants Debbie Liston to quit skating, look at Mary. Or look at Mary's father. He figures to pay out something like a hundred thousand dollars over the next five or ten years to make Mary into the champion she ain't ever gonna be. And the reason she won't ever make it is that she had the misfortune to come along at the same time as Debbie Liston."

"They compete in the same events?"

"Well, no," he said. "I just used Mary for illustration. Actually, she and Debbie get along real well. But you get my meaning."

"Yes."

He put his arm around my shoulder. We were pals now.

"I figure it's worth a pretty good piece of change to me to find out if there's something to worry about," he said. "Frankly, I hope you're right—that it's some kid at school getting some cheap laughs. I can handle that. But I'd like to know."

Well, now. I'd be doing the man a favor.

"I charge three-fifty a day, plus expenses. And I'll need something up front."

"I'll write you a check," he said. "How much?"

I considered it. "A thousand."

He nodded. "Back in a minute."

I returned to the two women. "I'll give it a try," I said. "See what I can come up with. But I need some

which is more than I can say for those merit scholars I got out there tending the snack bar." He gave me a world-weary shrug and a grin and pulled out a check-book from the center drawer of his desk. "A thousand you said, right?"

"Right."

He clasped a felt-tip pen and scribbled a check. Then he meticulously filled in the stub before tearing out the check and handing it to me.

"Anything else I can do for you?"

"You could tell me how to find Philip Lanham."

"I'll take a look," he said. He swiveled around to a card file on the shelf behind him.

"I was wondering if Irene would tell you about Philip," he said, rummaging through the file. "If you ask me, this sort of thing isn't his style. Nice kid."

"That's what Jane Borman said, too."

"Well, you gotta check it out, I guess," he said. He pulled a card from the file and inspected it before handing it to me. Then he gave me a blank card to write on.

"This address isn't right anymore," he said. "I remember his parents moved to the West Coast a year or so ago. Philip lives with somebody else now. I forget who."

"Isn't that unusual? The parents move away, and they leave their fifteen-year-old behind?"

"Happens oftener than you'd think. Besides, Philip's seventeen, and he'd practically moved out of the house anyway. Skating takes up a lot of time if you're serious about it."

"So I gather. Any idea where I can find him?"

"He doesn't come here anymore. You could try Springfield Arena out in Virginia. I heard he skates there."

I copied that address on the card too and slipped the card into my shirt pocket with the check.

"I'll probably be around a lot in the next few days," I said.

"I'll let my people know so they won't keep trying to charge you admission," he said.

He stood up to shake my hand. There was a photograph on the wall behind his desk, a framed black-and-white glossy of a skating couple. The boy seemed to be pivoting on the toe of one skate. With his outstretched arm he supported the girl in a position that was nearly parallel to the ice, except that her head dipped below the line of her torso until it almost touched the surface.

Dumas's glance followed mine.

"That's a death spiral," he said. "It's a required move in pairs competition, and it's real pretty when it's done well. You oughta see Debbie and Phil . . . Jerry do it."

"I think I've seen that picture before," I said.

He glanced at it again, and an expression I couldn't quite place crossed his face.

"It's a familiar angle," he said. "You see pictures just like it in all the programs for the professional ice shows."

"I haven't been to an ice show since I was a kid."

He looked at the picture again. "I don't know then. Newspaper, maybe." He turned and clapped me on the shoulder. "I'll show you out," he said.

He led me back toward the front door. He moved fast for a big man, and I had to hurry to keep up with him.

He stopped about fifty feet from the front door. "Here come Debbie and Jerry," he said. "Want to meet them?"

"Not yet. Maybe tomorrow."

We stood aside as they entered. I would have recognized Irene Liston's daughter anywhere. The mahogany hair was cut short, rather than long like her mother's, but otherwise it was the same face. There was a slight upturn to her nose, which her mother didn't have, and her eyes might have been infinitesimally bluer, but otherwise they could have been the same person at different stages of life. She wore the regulation gear of a well-to-do Washington teenager—faded jeans, Reeboks, and a blue-and-yellow ski parka—but she had the face of a woman.

"She must have inherited the nose from her father," I said.

"I wouldn't know. Her father died before she was born."

The boy was dark-haired, also, and slight of build, with a prominent Adam's apple. He had the gawky look that boys sometimes get when their voices start to change.

Dumas read my mind. "He's only a year older than Debbie," he said quietly. "At that age, girls mature faster."

"About ten years faster," I said. I watched them as they passed us—the sixteen-year-old boy and the fifteen-year-old woman—and marveled at how seldom men and women arrive at the same place at the same time.

"If you're coming back to meet them tomorrow," Dumas said, "you probably ought to get here about five-thirty. That's when they start practice."

"Five-thirty in the morning?"

"I know. It's a long day for them, too."

We shook hands again, and I headed for the front door. As I passed through I caught a quick, unwanted glimpse of my reflection in the glass.

Dumas was right; I looked young. They tell you it's an advantage to look young, but that's only true when you're old. I was approaching thirty, and I still looked like a teenager. Even the beard I had grown to make me look older had had the effect of heightening the look of callow youth. It hadn't grown right, for one thing; it filled out fine around the chin and sideburns but dwindled to a few wisps of fuzz along the jawline. It was the kind of beard Debbie Liston's partner might have grown.

All I needed were zits.

I stepped through the door into the December cold. A little distance away an automobile engine started up, and a yellow Toyota sedan eased out of a parking space. The driver was clean-shaven and had hair that could have been either blond or gray. A pair of foam rubber dice was slung over the rearview mirror, and the car sported a good-size dent on the left front fender. I made a mental note of the number on the license plate as the car eased out into the traffic and drove away.

Chapter Two

The cab that stopped for me on Connecticut Avenue was driven by a grizzly bear who was pumping thick blue smoke out of the bowl of a stumpy briar. Hung from the back of the front seat, where no paying passenger could miss it, was a sign printed in block letters on white cardboard. It read: THANK YOU FOR NOT SMOKING.

"This your cab or do you just rent it?" I asked the bear.

"Made the last payment in October. Why?"

"So you make the policies, right? About smoking, for instance?"

"Pipe smoking's not smoking," he said. "Pipes smell good. Besides, I didn't make the rule for me."

He craned his neck and peered at me through the rearview mirror. "Don't I know you from someplace?"

"I don't think so."

"Sports," he said. "High school, I think. You pitched for Woodrow Wilson."

"You've got a good memory. That was nearly twelve years ago."

"I used to follow the high schools," he said. "I had two kids that played, so I went to a lot of games.

Besides, you were good. I sort of figured you for a major-league prospect. You were scouted a little, I remember."

"I sort of figured me for a major-league prospect, too."

"So what happened?"

"I went the way of all fastballers," I said. "I just went there a lot faster than some."

"So what do you do now?"

"I'm self-employed," I said.

When I had first gone to work as a private investigator, my sister Susan had said, "Leo, some people trade in their cars every few years. You trade in your whole career."

It was late afternoon, and we were going against the rush-hour traffic, but the going was still slow. A light rain had begun falling, and it gradually turned to snow as we inched our way along. In Washington, any form of winter precipitation ties up traffic in all directions.

I paid the cabbie a few blocks from my office and walked the rest of the way. The snow was getting heavier, and I had to squint to keep from getting an eyeful. The rock salt crunched under my feet, and the wind carried the scent of fresh popcorn from a store along F Street. Christmas was still three weeks away, but it was beginning to seep into my bones.

My office was on the third floor of a building that had seen better days, although even its best days probably weren't all that good. There was an elevator, but a quick glance would convince you not to put your trust in it, and you would be right. I always used the stairs.

Georgie was cleaning off her desk when I walked in. She had bought a roll of paper towels from a store down the street and was furiously scrubbing the wood-grain plastic with water and dish detergent. She looked up and grinned at me, brushing one strawberry-blond wisp of hair out of her eyes.

"And to think I came to work for you to get away from housework," she said.

"Looks good, though. You do windows, too?"

She stuck her tongue out at me. I passed on into my office. I called a friend in the sports department at the *Post,* and he turned me over to another reporter who covered figure skating when he wasn't covering schoolboy basketball. The reporter, whose name was Roger, remembered Debbie Liston.

"I saw her compete a couple of times," he said. "She was in Winston-Salem last year and almost went all the way. I think she's got a new partner now, and that might set her back some."

"Do you remember her partner?"

"Old partner or new one?"

"Old one."

"Philip something. Hang on a minute." I could hear paper rustling. "Yeah, Philip Lanham. Tall kid, lanky, bright red hair, must have been a foot and a half taller than Debbie. They looked a little funny together, and that probably hurt them with the judges."

"Does something like that make a difference?"

"Listen, in figure skating, looks are everything. Well, not really everything, but a lot. The Russians, now, used to do it all the time. They'd put an eleven-year-old girl with a sixteen-year-old boy, so the boy could throw her around easier. But that's not the American style. Over here they go more for balance."

"That's why there's so much emphasis on costumes. Looks."

"Oh, yeah. And the judges are very conservative. Ever see a figure skater with a nose ring?"

"Not that I recall."

"You won't, either. Tennis is supposed to be a conservative sport, but it's not as conservative as figure skating."

After I hung up, I called a friend in the motor vehicle department. The yellow Toyota I had seen at the rink was registered to someone named Henry Schneider, who lived on Euclid Place.

The name meant nothing to Irene Liston or Jane Borman.

"Should I know him?" Jane asked when I called her.

"I don't know. A man answering the description you gave me was driving away, in a car that matched the description you gave me, as I left the rink today. The car is registered to Henry Schneider."

"Well, it isn't a name I recognize," she said.

"When does Debbie skate in public again?" I asked. "If these threats are real, I'd like to know how much time we have."

"The regionals are two weeks off, in Atlantic City," she said. "But she and Jerry will be participating in an exhibition on Saturday."

"This is Monday. We don't have much time."

I hung up and retrieved a Washington, D.C., street map from my desk. Euclid Place turned out to be in

Adams Morgan, a neighborhood north of Dupont Circle and the embassy district.

I put the map in my pocket. I would go there later. First I would go in search of Philip Lanham, boy figure skater and potential extortionist.

The skating rink to which Philip Lanham had retreated was in Springfield, a suburban community in Virginia about fifteen miles outside the District. The rink was newly built and still smelled of new paint and plastic.

Lanham was in the center of the ice when I arrived, practicing spins. I watched from the sidelines for a few minutes, until it became apparent that he wasn't coming in for a while. I found the rental counter and rented a pair of skates for myself.

The skates felt strange. I learned to skate as a child, like most people, but I had never tried it before on figure skates. Whenever I got crouched in skating position, I felt myself pitching forward. After a couple of spills, I got the knack of leaning backward to counteract the tendency to pitch forward, but it was a funny way to skate. More than that, it was a decidedly uncomfortable position.

I skated a couple of laps around the rink to regain my bearings, keeping an eye on Lanham as I did so. Eventually he left center ice and began skating around the oval with the crowd. I fell in alongside.

"This is hard work," I said.

He grinned at me.

"You're fighting too hard," he said. "Quit leaning so far back."

"If I don't lean backward I'll fall on my face," I said.

"I bet you play hockey," he said.

"I learned to skate on hockey skates. Lot of years ago, though."

"That's what I figured," he said. "It's a whole different feel on hockey skates. You don't have the support you need. I tried skating on them and nearly killed myself. They're a menace to humanity."

He was expressing my own sentiments about the figure skates I was wearing, but it didn't seem appropriate to say so. Instead, I said, "How do I skate in these things?"

"Straighten up," he said. "Get out of that crouch. Keep your rear over your skates at all times. Ever go skiing? Downhill, I mean?"

"Yeah."

"Same knee action," he said. "You want soft knees. Helps you hold your edges and smooths out the bumps and ruts in the ice."

"I'll try it," I said. "And I appreciate it."

"A lot of people make the same mistakes," he said. "You get to where you can spot the beginners."

"Are you Philip Lanham?"

The grin vanished. "Who wants to know?"

"My name's Leo McFarlin," I said. "I'm a private investigator. I came out here to find you. I'd like to talk to you for a few minutes."

"About what?"

"Debbie Liston."

"I got nothing to say. What do you want to know about her?"

"Somebody's been threatening to kill her," I said. "I've been hired to figure out why."

We had been slowing down as we talked. Now he came to a halt, nearly bring down a couple of elderly women who had been tailgating. He turned and faced me.

"Who hired you?" he asked.

"Irene Liston. Debbie's mother."

"And naturally she mentioned me."

"She said you might have a reason to be angry."

"Not with Debbie. With Irene."

"Tell me about it."

"Let's get off the ice," he said.

We were near the exit. Lanham stepped briskly off the ice and onto the rubber matting. I toddled after him as he strode to the lobby. He passed through it and stopped at a swinging door on the other side.

"This is a team room," he said. "We can talk in here."

He motioned me through ahead of him, and I took a seat on a rough wooden bench. He sat facing me in the tiny room. I wondered how they ever managed to squeeze an entire hockey team into such a tight space.

Even sitting down he looked tall. I guessed he was about six-four. He had an angular face, with planes and facets like a diamond. The red hair—almost orange, actually—was parted in the center and was cut stylishly. The deep-green sweater he was wearing looked like cashmere.

"How does a struggling amateur skater support himself while he struggles?" I asked.

"Meaning how much of my income comes from ex-tortion?"

"Meaning, how does a struggling skater support himself. That's all."

"With difficulty." He let a strained smile slip out. "I get some money from my parents. Not a lot, be-cause they're not well off. My coach pays me a little for doing odd jobs around her house. Actually, she pays me in lessons. I have a part-time job after school, and I board with my coach. It's tough."

"Sounds hard."

"It *is* hard," he said. "Some kids have angels—se-cret backers who contribute to their support because they have potential. Not me."

"Does Debbie have an unknown benefactor?"

"Well, he's hardly unknown," he said. "The senator seems to be paying most of her bills. Irene doesn't talk about it, but everybody knows about it."

"Senator who?"

"Hollister is his name. I think he's from Nebraska, or someplace."

"Missouri," I said. "I've met him. What's his con-nection to Debbie?"

"Irene works for him on the Hill. I hear they're very close."

He looked at me expectantly, as if I were supposed to be shocked. I ignored it.

"Tell me about your breakup with Debbie," I said.

"Why don't you ask Irene?"

"She can only tell me her side of it," I said. "I've heard that. Now I want to hear yours."

He considered that, then nodded. "It happened very

quickly. There isn't much to say. Irene told me herself."

"No warning that it was coming?"

He shook his head. "I got to the rink one day about fifteen minutes early, but Debbie wasn't there. Neither was Jane. Irene said Debbie wasn't feeling well. Then she sat me down and said she wanted to talk to me, that I wasn't working out, that I just wasn't able to keep up with Debbie's progress. Something like that."

"What was your reaction to that?"

"I was stunned. She was talking pure foolishness, of course, and I think she knew it. If anything, I'm a better skater than Debbie is."

"Did you say anything?"

"Nothing effective. To tell you the truth, I didn't take it all in at the time."

"Why wasn't Jane there when this was going on?"

"I wondered about that myself," he said. "Irene may have asked her to stay away. She gives in to Irene on a lot of things anyway."

"Did you try to talk to her later?"

"I tried. I called her up the next day, but she wouldn't come to the phone, and she wouldn't return my calls. Shortly after that, Irene called me at home and told me never to call Jane, or Debbie, or her, ever again. She said she'd call the police and complain that I was harassing them. That was her word, harassing."

"So what did you do?"

"I tried to call Debbie," he said.

"In spite of the warning?"

He shrugged. "She wouldn't call the police over

something like that. She'd look silly, and Irene doesn't like to look silly."

"Did you reach Debbie?"

The hesitation was so slight I almost didn't notice. "She never answered, and she never called back. After a while I gave up."

I changed the subject. "I gather you don't think much of Irene's reasons for firing you."

"They're nonsense, like I said. Debbie was holding *me* back, if anything."

"You know that?"

"I know it, Debbie knows it, Jane knows it, even Irene knows it. She won't admit it, but she knows it."

"Then why *did* she dump you?"

He gave me a quick, mirthless grin. "Because she thought Debbie and I were getting too close to each other, too involved. She thought it might interfere with her plans. She wants to make Debbie champion of the world, and she won't rest until she does."

"Were you and Debbie in love?"

"Yes."

"It was a mutual feeling?"

"Yes."

"Then why didn't Debbie return your calls?"

"Because she was scared," he said. "Debbie is afraid of her mother. Never forget that. She responds to Irene the way a lion responds to its trainer in the circus. Irene Liston is a bully."

"But you're not afraid of her?"

"I'm a seventeen-year-old male figure skater, Mr. McFarlin. I've been fighting bullies all my life."

* * *

It was long after sunset when I finally found the house on Euclid Place. The house was dark, and the yellow Toyota was nowhere in sight. I parked farther down the street and waited for someone to show up.

In its youth, the house had probably been dark-red brick, but the bricks had been painted white some years ago and now the white was dirty. It looked almost yellow in the light of the street lamp. It was a small row house on a corner lot, with a high stoop and a separate entrance to the half basement underneath.

The backyard was enclosed by a high board fence that reminded me of center field in an old minor league ballpark. I had seen a lot of those in my life. These days you find board fences mostly in the minors; major league teams tend to play in converted football stadiums, where the outfield fences are all temporary arrangements that come down at the end of the season.

I waited for about an hour, but no one showed up. I remembered that I had planned to get to the skating rink early the next morning, so I made a U-turn and drove slowly past the house on my way home.

Chapter Three

I was up and about at four-thirty the next morning, even though the sun wasn't. After breakfast I drove to the rink.

Someone had put up Christmas decorations since I had been there the day before: molded red plastic candles with garish orange flames, sprinkled with some sort of silvery glitter. The candles sat in the middle of the lobby. Across one wall, a huge pasteboard Santa grinned at me from the front seat of a sleigh pulled by three cutesy-pie reindeer, one of which had a red nose. An electric motor had been connected to Santa's upraised arm, making him appear to wave. I waved back to be polite.

Jane Borman was on the ice talking to two teenagers who had their backs to me. She saw me over their shoulders, smiled, and wiggled her fingers in greeting. The teenagers swiveled to look.

They all met me at the entrance to the ice.

"This is the man I was telling you about," she said to the teenagers. "Mr. McFarlin, meet Debbie and Jerry."

"Call me Leo," I said.

"Is Debbie really in danger?" the boy asked. He had a voice to fit his face: high-pitched and adenoidal.

"That's what I'm here to find out," I said.

I had to admit, having now seen them both up close, that Debbie's new skating partner was a closer match, in terms of height and coloring, than her old one. Her new partner was maturing at a far slower pace, however, and he had the gangly, loose-limbed look of a high school sprinter. Debbie, on the other hand, looked even more like an adult than she had the previous day.

"Do you want to take them somewhere and talk to them privately?" Jane asked.

"Just Debbie right now," I said.

"You can use the team rooms or Jack's office if you like."

"The bench over there in the corner will do nicely."

Debbie walked ahead of me, balancing carefully on her thin steel blades. She was wearing a forest-green skating dress and green knitted leggings.

We sat together on the bench.

"Did Jane tell you why I'm here?" I asked.

"She said you were here to protect me," she said softly.

"First I want to determine if you need protection," I said. "Did you know that someone had threatened to kill you?"

"Jane told me."

"Does that surprise you?"

She nodded vigorously.

"Can you think of any reason why someone—any-one—might *want* to hurt you?"

"No."

"Can you think of any person who might believe he has reason to be angry with you? Regardless of whether the reason is realistic?"

"No."

"Someone you've had trouble with at school?"

"No."

"Someone following you on the street?"

"No."

"How about Philip?"

"No." But there was a flicker of something in her eyes. A flicker of . . . what? Fear?

"Are you sure?"

But the flicker, whatever it was, was gone. "I'm sure," she said.

"All right. I'd appreciate it if you'd think about this some more. Will you do that?"

"Yes."

"And if something occurs to you later, will you give me a call?"

"Yes."

I gave her one of my cards. "If I'm not around, leave word with my secretary. She'll know how to reach me."

She took the card without looking at it. "May I go now?"

"Sure. I'm through for the time being."

I watched her walk away from me, with her glossy hair bouncing gently, and wondered what a fifteen-year-old could have to lie about.

She joined her partner on the ice, gliding out to a point just off-center with one apparently effortless stroke. Jane spoke briefly to them and then skated away, leaving them alone on the ice. I met her as she came off.

"Did Debbie tell you anything useful?" she asked.

"I guess not. Still, I had to ask."

"They're about to run through their program now," she said. "Want to stay and watch?"

"Thanks."

She smiled and the little lines appeared again at the corners of her eyes. A flaw, to be sure, but a charming one.

"You must smile a lot," I said.

"I don't know. I hadn't thought about it. Why do you say that?"

"You seem to have it perfected," I said. "I don't think it could be done much better."

"Aren't you sweet," she said, and stepped past me on her way to a makeshift wooden booth a few feet away. Inside the booth was a small table that held a portable cassette tape recorder. A gray shielded cable led out of one end of the machine and snaked across the table to an old electronic amplifier. She removed a cassette from the pocket of her jacket and popped it into the recorder.

"This is their short program," she said. "We'll work on the long program later."

"What's a short program?"

She looked over her shoulder at me.

"Didn't you watch the Nagano Olympics? I thought everybody knew about that by now."

"My television doesn't work so well."

"Well, in pairs skating you have to perform two separate programs," she said. "One of them runs about two minutes, and the other runs about five." She tugged at the cable where it protruded from the amplifier.

"What's the difference, besides the fact that one's longer than the other?"

"In the short program," she said, "you have to perform certain required moves—a specific jump, a specific spin, a certain kind of death spiral. In the longer program the point is to put together the most expressive combination, so you have more leeway. You choose the moves you want to do, as long as they're of a high-enough level of difficulty, and you put them together the way you prefer."

She had set up a portable video recorder and camera on a tripod nearby. She went to the camera, peered through the viewfinder, and fiddled briefly with the focus.

"Do me a favor?"

"Sure," I said.

"Look through here and keep the camera on Debbie and Jerry while I start the music."

"All right."

The tiny video screen in the viewfinder gave the kids a dreamy look, all blacks and whites like a distant memory. There was a crackling sound in the loudspeakers overhead, and an orchestra burst into the opening strains of the overture to *Gypsy*.

Debbie and Jerry, hands linked, glided away from their starting point. I concentrated on following them through the viewfinder. It wasn't easy, for they moved quickly.

The orchestra concluded its opening motif and

swung into "Everything's Coming Up Roses." Almost immediately, Jerry took Debbie by the waist and lifted her an arm's length over his head. She spun in the air at least twice, and he set her down gently on the ice again, as easily as if he were setting down a crystal wineglass. They had not slackened speed.

"Sloppy," Jane said.

"Looked good to me."

She shook her head. "They've got two minutes to work in five required moves, make them fit the music, and make them look natural. That lift didn't look natural."

"I'll take your word for it."

"That's why I tape their practices," she said. "I'll play it back for them later, and they can see what went wrong."

I moved away from the camera and let her take over. Debbie and Jerry were performing some sort of footwork on the ice, hand-in-hand at full speed, nearly the full length of the ice away from us. Then they disengaged and leaped together, landing in a pair of matched arabesques and spinning in perfect unison.

"What do you call that maneuver?"

"Flying camels," Jane said. "But not very good ones. Look how Debbie's free leg is drooping. She's not concentrating."

They completed their spins and skated back toward center ice.

"Now the death spiral," Jane said.

The mood of the music changed. The tempo slowed. Jerry turned to face his partner, took her left hand, and led her into a circle of ever-tightening radius. She leaned back into the circle. I recalled the picture I had seen in Jack Dumas's office, and it occurred to me that there was considerable resemblance between the couple in the picture and this pair of teenagers. It was more than a similarity in the maneuver; it was a physical resemblance. Not exact but very close.

Jane was standing beside me, peering through the viewfinder and chewing her lower lip.

There was a sickening crack on the ice. I turned quickly to see Debbie Liston sliding slowly across the ice on her back. Her eyes were closed, and she was still and quiet.

"Debbie!" Jane yelled frantically. She punched the button and stopped the tape.

In the sudden silence we could hear the steel clatter of a skate blade as it skittered across the ice and kissed the barrier at our feet. It was not attached to the boot.

"Oh, no!" Jane yelled. "She's hurt."

Debbie lay on the ice without moving. Her eyes were closed. I thought I could see her breathing, but I was too far away to be certain.

I sprinted for the doorway that led to the ice. My basketball sneakers gripped the ice better than I had expected, although my feet were cold through the rubber soles.

Jerry was kneeling over Debbie, peering into her face, by the time I arrived.

"She's dead," he said. There were tears welling in his eyes.

I felt her pulse. It was strong and regular, and she was obviously breathing. I could even see her carotid artery throbbing.

"She isn't dead," I said. "I don't think she's hurt bad, but I can't be sure. She hit her head pretty hard by the sound of it."

"Yes."

"There could have been a concussion. Better call an ambulance."

He nodded excitedly and skated off toward the exit. I returned my attention to Debbie. Her pulse remained strong, and she seemed to be breathing okay.

I could hear Jane skate to a stop behind me.

"Is she all right?"

"I think so. She hit her head pretty hard, though."

She touched my shoulder. "Oh, I was so scared."

"I know. Jerry's calling an ambulance. Did you see what happened? I wasn't watching at the time."

"They just fell," she said. "They were going into their death spiral when Jerry suddenly pitched forward and fell on top of her."

"Her skate blade must have broken under the weight," I said. "I saw it slide over there by the wall."

"Then there must be screws around somewhere, too. We'd better get them up before somebody trips over them."

She skated off toward where the skate blade lay and began peering at the ice. In a moment she was back.

"I found two screw heads," she said. "There are probably two more around here somewhere."

I took the two she had found, and she skated off to look for the others.

I compared the screw heads to the skate blade. The screws had broken cleanly away from the boot except for a small jagged stump on each one. The stump reminded me of a tree that had been felled by a beaver. On the underside of the steel plate that had connected the blade to the boot, I found fresh scratch marks as if someone had been scraping on it with a sharp nail. Or a metal file.

"I couldn't find any more screws," Jane said behind me. "They must be out there somewhere, though."

"I don't think so," I said. "I think they were removed before Debbie ever put on her skate."

"Why?"

"To ensure that the blade would break off," I said. "Somebody's been tampering with this skate."

"I wondered about that," she said. "I've seen skate blades break off before, but they usually take part of the sole of the boot with them when they go."

"Does Debbie take her skates home with her when she goes home or does she leave them in a locker?"

"She takes them home. They're big investments, and you want them where you can keep an eye on them."

"So nobody else would have access to them?"

She thought. "Well, there's Jack Dumas, I guess."

"Why Dumas?"

"Skates have to be sharpened. That isn't something Debbie can do for herself so Jack has been doing it for her. He keeps the skates here overnight when he does that."

"When were they last sharpened?"

"Last night," she said. "I remember Debbie complaining yesterday morning that one edge didn't feel right."

"So the skates were here last night. Where were they kept?"

"I suppose they're stored with the others," she said. "There's a workshop up front behind the rental counter."

"Is it kept locked?"

"I don't know. I suppose so. You'd have to ask Jack about that."

"I think I will," I said. "And this is as good a time as any."

I left Jane to wait for the ambulance while I went searching for Dumas. He wasn't in his office. There was a paper cup, half-filled with opaque coffee, on the windowsill. The coffee was cold and looked about as appetizing as recycled motor oil.

I sat down in a red plastic chair facing the desk and waited for Dumas to return. The room had a single window through which I could see wintry treetops and residential rooftops. Somewhere beyond the trees I could hear traffic sounds, the regular plopping sound of tires on concrete. The sound had a soothing effect on my nerves, like a cold compress on a migraine.

When he hadn't returned in fifteen minutes, I wandered back to the front of the rink. Debbie was conscious again and was sitting on a bench just off the ice. A couple of paramedics hovered over her. Jane saw me coming and met me halfway.

"They think she's okay, but they want to take her to the hospital and check her out," she said.

"That's probably wise," I said. "Did you find any more screw heads?"

"No, but I found this." She held up a large silver paper clip.

"Where did you find it?"

"Debbie was lying on it," she said. "She must have tripped on it, and she pulled Jerry down with her."

I took the paper clip from her. There was a notch in one end that could have been made by a skate blade.

"I wonder how it got there," I said.

She shrugged. "We find all sorts of things on the ice. After the public skating sessions we find a lot of change that falls out of people's pockets."

"You haven't had any public sessions today, have you? Not at five o'clock in the morning."

"No."

"And you have new ice since last night."

"It's been remade twice since the public session. They had an adult hockey game last night, and then they remade it again after the hockey game."

"So if the paper clip had been there last night, somebody might have tripped over it during the hockey game. And wouldn't it be frozen into the ice by now if it had been there that long?"

"I suppose so," she said. "But nobody has been on the ice today except us."

"Nobody?"

"Well, I guess Jack was there this morning. He usually goes out to inspect the surface first thing in the morning."

"Would he know Debbie and Jerry's program well enough to be sure of placing something in their path?"

"Jack?" I could see the idea was anathema to her. "He wouldn't do that. I don't know anybody who's more intent on seeing that Debbie and Jerry are successful."

"Somebody, apparently, wants them to fail."

"It can't be Jack," she said. "I'd be willing to believe it about anybody but Jack."

"You don't have to believe it," I said. "Just think about it. Would it have been possible for him to place that paper clip so Debbie would be certain to fall?"

She thought about it.

"No," she said. "I mean yes, it would be possible, but only barely. You couldn't count on it. He couldn't be certain that they would cross over the precise spot he had chosen. They're supposed to cross the same place every time they do their program, but they're human like the rest of us. They never do it quite the same every time."

"All the same," I said, "it would be worth a try. If they missed the paper clip, he could just pick it up and try again some other time."

"That's horrible," she said.

"Yes, it is," I said. "I hope I'm wrong. Have you seen him this morning?"

"No. Wasn't he in his office?"

"No."

"Sometimes he goes home for a few hours in the mornings," she said. "He works an eighteen-hour day here, and he has to take his breaks when he can. Things are usually slow in the mornings."

"Where does he live?"

"I don't have his address," she said. "I think Ray Martin does. He's the older fellow out front, at the skate rental counter."

Martin turned out not to be that old, but his gray hair and craggy face made him look more ancient than he probably was. It was only on second glance that I noticed the firm jawline had not yet begun to go to jowl. Early to middle forties, I guessed.

It took some persuading to get him to give me Dumas's address, but finally he pulled out a green card file and located the address for me.

"Jack'll have my job for this," he said, writing out the information for me.

"I won't tell him where I got it."

The address was in the Maryland suburbs, not far away.

"What kind of car does he drive?" I asked.

"A Volkswagen Rabbit," Martin said. "It's that lime-green color that was so popular a few years back. If you see it in the parking lot, he's probably somewhere close by."

"If he comes back, will you tell him that I'd like to talk to him?"

"I'm going off duty myself in ten minutes. I don't think I'll see him, but I'll tell him if I do."

I stopped by Dumas's office again before I left, but he hadn't returned. As I stood in the doorway I realized that something about the room itself had been bothering me. Something I couldn't put my finger on.

I stared at the room for a couple of minutes trying to identify the problem. The cup of coffee remained on the windowsill, untouched since my previous visit. The ancient typewriter still sat on a corner of the shabby desk. The plastic chair I had sat in remained where I had left it.

The difference, I realized finally, was the picture on the wall. When I had been there the day before, there had been a black-and-white photograph of two skaters performing a death spiral. Now the wall displayed a color picture of the Lincoln Memorial. It was smaller than the other photograph, and I could see the faded outline of the larger frame behind it.

Chapter Four

Outside, the sun was up. Instead of cloudy-bright, which is the way the weather had been most of the week, it was turning to cloudy-dull. The sun was a dim silver ball shining through the thin cloud cover, and I could see heavy, sodden gray clouds moving in from the southeast. Snow was coming. Again.

There was no lime-green Volkswagen in the parking lot.

It took me about thirty minutes in the mid-morning traffic to reach Dumas's house. It was a pleasant, boxy red-brick house on a corner lot, the sort of house that a realtor might describe as a "starter" house, neglecting to mention that it "started" at a hundred thousand dollars.

There were three steps to the concrete slab that served as a front porch. I stood on the porch, flanked by struggling forsythia, and pushed the doorbell button. Somewhere inside I heard it ring. There was no response.

When there was still no answer after two more rings, I decided to look around.

In back, a steep driveway plunged downward to a cramped garage. The house had been built, and then the garage, and then a later owner, probably, had built the screened-in porch that perched atop the garage. I peeped through the row of windows at the top of the overhead door and saw a sawhorse, an aluminum extension ladder, a pile of dusty rags, some lumber, and a power lawn mower in a corner. There was no car.

I walked back up the driveway and looked into the screened-in back porch. There was the usual sort of furniture: a couple of wicker chairs, a wrought-iron outdoor coffee table, a matching bench.

I reached for the doorknob and discovered that the door was already ajar, and there were pry marks on the doorjamb as if someone had forced it open. I pushed the door gently with my knuckles and stepped inside.

Just inside the door was a small kitchen equipped with tired appliances that were turning yellow with age. Green and yellow curtains framed the window. A drying rack sat on the drain board near the sink, and a plastic dish and a coffee cup sat gathering dust on the rack. A yellow steel bread box sat on the counter nearby, and an electric drip coffeemaker rubbed shoulders with it. A place for everything, and everything more or less in its place.

The dining room lay through an open arch. An imitation oak sideboard hulked against one wall. A walnut-veneer dining table monopolized the middle of the floor. It was a cheap table, probably meant to occupy an eat-in kitchen rather than a formal dining room. It was the sort of furniture that might have been supplied by a rental company.

The entire house, in fact, had the feel of rented lodgings. There were plastic wood-grain surfaces on the furniture to hide the particle board beneath. Cheap carpets covered the floor.

Odder still was the absence of personal effects. The pictures on the wall were the sort of prints that come in the frames you buy at discount stores. There were no snapshots, seashell collections, ashtrays from Ixtapa. There were no signs of a woman in his life. There were, in fact, no signs of a life in his life.

Upstairs it was a bit better. A spare bedroom had been outfitted as an office with a wobbly wooden desk, a typewriter that could have been a twin of the one at the skating rink, and several rows of books on tax accounting, bookkeeping, and commercial law.

A color poster had been tacked to one wall: Dorothy Hamill in mid-spin, head laid back, arms raised halfway. The poster was creased, and there were staple holes in the center. A picture torn from a magazine or an ice show souvenir program wasn't exactly the same as a snapshot of Mom and Dad on their trip to the Grand Canyon, but it was at least a personal touch of sorts.

There was a mail clip on the desk, and I glanced through it quickly. Among the letters was a white window envelope addressed to John J. Dumas and bearing the return address of a newspaper in Rochester, New York. The envelope contained a bill for twenty-five dollars for a classified advertisement and a rental charge for a box number. The advertisement had been clipped from the paper and taped to the bottom half of the bill:

INFORMATION PLEASE

  *For a book in progress, I am seeking infor-
mation about figure skaters who competed in the
Rochester area during the late 1970s. I am particularly interested in pairs skaters. Please con-
tact Box 50A.*

I copied the phone number of the newspaper from
the envelope and returned the bill to its proper place.

Someone else, apparently, had been looking around
Dumas's office. The filing cabinet in the corner had
been pried open, the lock popped. I looked through
the file but found mostly rink records that I didn't
understand.

On my way back to the rink I stopped at a bank
and got several dollars in change. Then I found a telephone booth and placed a call to Rochester. I got
through to the newspaper accounting department right
away, and a pleasant young male voice asked if it
could help me.

"I'm trying to update my records," I said. "Can you
search your files and tell me whether you received my
check? I had a classified ad running in your personals
column a couple of weeks ago."

"Name please?"

"Dumas."

"One moment, sir."

He was back quickly.

"John J. Dumas?"

"That's right."

"Yes, sir. We received your check on . . . December
first."

"Thank you," I said. "Guess I'm getting kinda behind in my records."

"I understand how that can happen, sir. Anything else we can do for you? Care to renew your listing?"

"Not just now," I said. "But would you mind checking my box to see if there's anything in it?"

"Be right back," he said.

When he returned, he said, "There is a letter, sir. The return address says it's from a Mrs. Eloise Leitner in Irondequoit. That's a little northeast of here, up along the lakefront."

"Could you read me the letter?"

"You mean over the phone? We're not permitted to do that, sir."

"I realize it's not your standard procedure," I said, "but I'm kind of in a hurry. My book is on deadline, and this letter may contain just the information that's been holding me up."

"The letter will be forwarded to you today, sir. You should have it tomorrow, or the day after."

"I understand that, but I've got to get the book off to the publisher today."

He was weakening. "I could lose my job."

"I promise they won't hear about it from me," I said.

"Well . . ."

"And I really need that information."

"All right," he said. "Let me open it." I heard the sound of paper ripping.

"Actually," he said finally, "it's a very short letter. It probably won't help you much."

"What does it say?"

"It says: 'To whom it may concern. In the late seventies and early eighties I was extremely active as a skating coach in the Rochester area. For three years I coached two of the finest pairs skaters the area has ever produced. Their names were Irene Kreeger and Harry Liston. Although Harry Liston is now deceased, and I have lost track of Irene Kreeger, my memories of them are strong. I would be happy to discuss them with you. You may reach me at the address above. Sincerely, Eloise Leitner.' "

Bingo.

"Is it any help to you?" I heard him say.

"Very much," I said. "Could you give me that address again?"

The Richard B. Russell Senate Office Building stands at the corner of Delaware and Constitution Avenues. It was there that I found Sen. Hollister's office.

When you see a senator's office in the movies there's always a view of the Capitol through the window behind his desk. In real life such views are hard to come by. Sen. Wellington Hollister, by virtue of seniority and other things, had managed to come by one of them. He had a corner office on the third floor behind a massive wooden door that bore a carved, enameled replica of the Missouri state seal.

Behind the door a glassy-eyed receptionist asked whom I wished to see and then dialed two digits with a perfectly manicured finger. Somewhere back in the rabbit warren of partitioned office spaces I heard a phone ringing. The receptionist murmured something softly into the receiver and then told me, in her zombie voice, that Mrs. Liston would be right with me.

And she was.

"Good morning, Mr. McFarlin. Won't you come this way."

I followed her past filing cabinets and photocopy machines. She wore a knitted suit that made her movements seem almost liquid as she walked. She stopped at the door to Hollister's office.

"The senator is in a committee hearing right now," she said. "We can talk in here."

I sat on a leather sofa, and she sat in a nearby armchair. The office was about five times the size of the reception area. Photographs hung from the wall in dime store frames: the senator with Ted Kennedy, with Jimmy Carter, with Bill Clinton, with Stan Musial. The paraphernalia of public life. The lights were turned off at the moment, but I doubted that the room would have seemed much brighter if they had been on. During my brief stint as a newspaper reporter on Capitol Hill I had noticed that Congressional offices always seemed gloomy, even on sunny days.

"I talked to Jane this morning," Mrs. Liston said. "She told me what happened to Debbie. She doubts that it was an accident, and I had the distinct impression that she had gotten that idea from you."

"The paper clip on the ice could have been an accident," I said. "But the screws had been worked on with a metal file or a hacksaw."

"I see," she said.

"And then there are the threats. The reason you hired me."

"I hadn't forgotten," she said. "I confess I haven't put much store by them up to now. I assumed you'd discover they were some sort of prank."

"And now?"

"Now, I don't know," she said. "I dislike Philip, as you know, but I find it hard to believe he would do something vicious. He hasn't the fortitude."

"Are there no other possible suspects in your mind?"

"Do *you* have another?"

"How about Jack Dumas?"

The idea took a second to register with her. "Jack? You can't be serious."

"Dumas is the one who sharpened Debbie's skates last night," I said. "She had her fall this morning. The tampering had been done recently."

She nodded, thinking. "Still," she said, "the skates were in the pro shop all night. Anyone could get to them."

"Anyone who worked there," I said. "I don't see someone wandering in off the street, walking behind the counter in the pro shop, and tampering with a pair of skates without attracting attention."

"There are other employees," she said.

"What about Ray Martin?" I said. "He seems to be second in command."

"I don't believe I know him," she said. "Is he an employee?"

"Gray hair, blue eyes, kind of long-faced, forties."

She hesitated, but shook her head. "If he works a day shift I probably wouldn't run into him."

"Point two," I said. "Dumas makes the ice every

morning. Shortly after he did that, the paper clip was found on the ice in a strategic spot."

"I see," she said. "What does Jack say to this? Or haven't you asked him?"

"I intend to ask him," I said, "just as soon as I find him."

"He isn't at the rink?"

"Or at home," I said. "Of course, for all I know, he could be out Christmas shopping. It's just that he's disappeared at a particularly inopportune time."

"I see what you mean," she said. "It does look rather bad for him, doesn't it?"

"I can't rule him out, anyway."

"I don't understand why he would try to harm Debbie, though," she said.

"I don't understand why *anyone* would want to harm Debbie," I said. "That's what has bothered me about this case since I agreed to take it. Why would anyone care whether Debbie skates in competition or not? Who could possibly profit if she doesn't?"

"Does the reason matter?"

"If I knew the reason, I might know how to stop whatever is going on," I said. "If I *knew* what was going on."

"Perhaps."

I took a deep breath. "There's something else that makes me wonder about Dumas. He seems to be checking up on you."

"On me? You mean he's spying on me? Having me followed? That sort of thing?"

"Not exactly. He seems to be making inquiries into your past. Maybe he's trying to gain some sort of leverage, so he can blackmail you into taking Debbie out of competition."

Her mouth made little chewing motions, as if she were working a particularly tough piece of meat. "How do you mean?" she asked.

"He seems to be asking about your skating career."

She chuckled, but there was no mirth in it. "My brief skating career."

"Is there anything in it that might provide someone with some leverage?"

Her eyes seemed focused in the middle distance, as if she were watching a movie screen where her life story was playing.

"Well, there's something, I suppose," she said finally. "It isn't that I couldn't bear it if it came out, but it was a bit sordid. And embarrassing."

"Want to tell me about it?"

She thought it over. "I guess it can't hurt," she said. "And perhaps the information will be useful to you."

She settled back in the armchair. "This is not the most pleasant part of my life we're discussing here," she said.

No response seemed required, so I didn't offer one.

"I was young, then. Nearly as young as Debbie is now. I did . . . foolish things, I suppose. I don't know if I'd do them differently today. I suppose they wouldn't be considered quite so foolish today, but the world was different then."

"When was this?"

"Oh, the early eighties. About nineteen eighty-three, I guess."

"You were in Rochester then?"

"Irondequoit. It's a suburban community north of Rochester."

"You were a pairs skater. Like Debbie."

"Yes. My name was Kreeger then. My partner's name was Harry. Harry Liston. We were very good. Isn't there a movie where one of the characters says that? I was good. I could have been a contenda.' "

"Marlon Brando in *On the Waterfront*. He was a fighter who took a dive because his brother told him to."

"Yes, well, we didn't take a dive. We fell in love instead. It had the same effect; it destroyed our careers."

"I don't understand."

"No, I suppose you don't. It's hard to understand unless you've been a competitive skater. When you're in competition, you can't afford distractions. You have no social life. You barely go to school. You're on the ice most of the day."

"Some people wouldn't put up with a life like that."

"We did," she said. Her lower lip trembled slightly. I could imagine her mentally calculating the precise rate of tremble that an onlooker would consider appropriate. Too little would go unnoticed. Too much would be melodramatic. She would know the difference.

"We tolerated the life because we had chosen it," she said. "It was *our* life. And there are . . . compensations. When you work so closely with someone, you develop a very intense relationship. You act alike, think alike, want the same things. It's a lot like marriage."

"But something happened to change your life."

She smiled. "Debbie happened."

"You got pregnant."

"Yes."

"And Harry was the father."

"Yes."

"So you were married."

"Very quickly. And quietly. And Debbie was born six months later. She was quite a lovely baby."

It was uncomfortable sitting in this private office, sharing Irene Liston's private reverie. I was getting impatient, the way I had in an earlier life on the days when I wasn't pitching.

"What did you do then?" I said. "You gave up your skating, I gather."

"Oh, there was never a possibility of ever resuming it. They weren't as liberal as all that in the eighties. I don't know that they are even today."

"So what did you *do?*"

"Harry dropped out of college and got a job driving a delivery truck," she said. "I tried working as a rink pro for a while, but we needed more money than I could make that way. I went to secretarial school."

"Where's your husband now?"

"He's dead," she said. "He died about three months later. He had been working late, and he was driving home, and he must have been very tired. He drove into a bridge abutment, and the gasoline tank exploded."

"I'm sorry."

"So am I. The honeymoon really wasn't over when

he died. I wonder sometimes if we would still be together today if he had lived. I think we would."

I thought her recitation had the sound of something she had memorized and told herself for a long time. Perhaps it was a form of consolation or justification.

"Where are your parents today?"

"My father died when I was twelve," she said. "My mother died soon after Harry and I were married. Before Harry, even."

"And Harry's parents?"

"Divorced years ago. Harry lived with his mother. Neither his father or mother cared very much for me, or for Harry for that matter."

"So what did you do after Harry's death?"

"I continued to work in Rochester for a while. Eventually I moved to Washington. I thought a secretary could probably make more money here than she could in Rochester. So far that's been the case."

"Who else might know your story? If Dumas wanted to find out about it, where could he go?"

"Our coach, I suppose. We were closer to her than to our parents, really."

"Eloise Leitner," I said.

"You've heard of her? She was a charming woman. I haven't seen her for fifteen years, though. I wonder if she's still alive."

"I believe she is," I said. "I can't imagine what sort of blackmail material someone might be able to find in what you've told me so far, though. Can you think of anything else?"

"Nothing," she said firmly. She stood up suddenly and smiled at someone over my shoulder.

"I'm sorry," she said. "We were just borrowing your office for a moment."

"It's all right, Irene," said a deep, familiar voice. "I didn't mean to barge in. Go right ahead and finish your conversation."

I turned to see Sen. Wellington Hollister standing in the doorway.

"We were just finishing," I said. "Thanks for your help, Mrs. Liston."

"Senator Hollister, this is Leo McFarlin," Irene Liston said.

"The senator and I have met before," I said.

Hollister nodded. "I was thinking your face was familiar. You're a reporter, aren't you? You interviewed me once." He gave me his politician's no-nonsense handshake and his politician's lopsided grin.

"It was a few years ago," I said. "You were on the special energy committee in those days."

"That's right," he said. "I had to give it up this year. The workload got to be too much. Old age, I guess."

He was fishing for a compliment. He didn't look as if old age was slowing him down at all. There was gray in his sideburns and creeping in at the temples, but he didn't look a day over forty-five, and I knew he was at least ten years older than that.

"Still a long way from senility," I said.

"Mr. McFarlin was on his way out," Irene said. "We'll let you have your office back now."

Hollister ignored her. "Are you still a reporter, Mr. McFarlin?" It was a pointed question: if I were, what was I doing talking privately with his personal secretary?

"Not anymore," I said. "I'm in business for myself."

"What sort of business?" He was trying to keep it light and mostly succeeding.

"You could call it the information business," I said.

"Mr. McFarlin is a private investigator," Irene said. "He's working for me."

Hollister's eyes widened a bit. "Is this about Debbie?" The question was directed to Irene, but he continued looking at me.

"Yes."

"Good, good," he said to me. "I wish you luck in catching whoever is doing this vicious thing."

"Thank you," I said.

"We think a lot of Debbie around here," he said. "And Irene, too."

I had already figured that out. I had seen the look that had passed between them as I shook Hollister's hand.

Hollister, I recalled, was divorced.

When I got back to the office, the afternoon mail was sitting on my desk. On top of the pile was a ivory-colored envelope with the name of a local law firm on it. I opened it and read it standing at the window, hoping it would be new business.

It wasn't.

My client, Ms. Hanson, has been extremely patient, but she feels her patience has been taxed unduly. You are, I am informed, six months overdue on your repayment of your loan. If payment is not forthcoming within sixty days, we shall be forced to take further action of a more drastic nature.

Oh, great. Lawyers, yet.

I walked into the front room. Georgie was sitting at her desk looking delectable.

"How much do I owe Susan now?" I asked.

She wrinkled her nose. "Five hundred and forty-two dollars. I remember because I just finished writing her a check this morning."

"So I'm on schedule?"

"Right on schedule."

"What do you make of this?" I handed her the letter.

I watched the frown begin. "It's some sort of joke," she said.

"If it is, I don't think she told her lawyer about it," I said, and went back to my office.

They were finally beginning to recognize my voice at the television newsroom where my sister worked, so they put me right through. Susan had developed an air of hearty worldliness fairly early in her television career, which, I suspected, made it easier to banter with the film crew while waiting for a couple of hours outside a closed-door meeting. Evidently she liked the sound of it because after a while she used it everywhere.

"Leo, it's good to hear from you. Are you calling to let me know you're alive or is there something I can do for you?"

"There's something you can do for me," I said. "You can call off your lawyer."

"What lawyer?"

"The one who's writing me threatening letters."

"Don't be silly, Leo. Lawyers don't write. They paste."

"This one writes," I said. "And he's threatening me with some sort of vague, lawyerly doom if I don't pay off your loan by yesterday morning."

I thought I heard honest puzzlement in her voice, but with Susan it was hard to tell. "You're kidding, of course."

"No, I'm not."

"Well, he isn't working for me. Does this lawyer have a name?"

I read her the name off the letter. There was a moment of silence, followed by a burst of contralto laughter.

"He did it," she said. "He did it. He really did it." More peals of laughter.

"Mind filling me in on the joke?"

"Yes, of course," she said, gasping. "I'm sorry. You must have been frightened when you got that letter."

"Well, concerned."

"I'm sure. Well, I met him at a party last week, at the Portuguese embassy. He's quite important, and I felt a very strong attraction to him. He's so earnest, mature, sincere, a fascinating combination. Sort of a combination of Paul Newman and Henry Kissinger."

"And rich?"

"Well off, certainly. That's part of what makes him so fascinating."

"Go on."

"Well, I think the attraction was mutual. So when he told me he would be happy to handle any legal business I might have—I mean, actually soliciting business—I was touched. They're not supposed to do that, you know. It was as if he were a knight, asking for a token to carry into battle. I felt an intense desire—a need, even—to find some legal work for him to do."

"And there I was, minding my own business."

"Well, in point of fact, Leo, your current business is minding everyone else's business, isn't it? So when you're minding your own business, you're actually . . ."

I sighed. "Go on with your story, please."

"Yes, I thought of you. I told him I had lent you money so you could go into business for yourself. Of course it didn't come out in the conversation that you were my brother, and since our names are different he wouldn't have known unless he had checked, and they never do that."

"So he patted you on the knee and said 'There, there, Daddy will get your money back.' Is that what happened?"

"Something like that," she said, and giggled. Imagine a foghorn giggling. "But don't worry, I'll call him off. I'll tell him you paid up or something."

"Actually, I owe you one more payment," I said, "but you'll get it next month right on time. Just call off your lap dog."

"He's more a tiger than a puppy," she said. "But I'll put a stop to it. Other than that, how are you doing, Leo?"

"Personally or professionally?"

"Either way."

"Vaguely discontented, personally. Happy enough, professionally. I have a client or two, and I'm making ends meet."

"Then I suppose there's no hope of persuading you to return to journalism?"

"Not just yet."

"Oh," she said. "Well, then," and hung up.

Chapter Five

"**J**im is really terribly embarrassed," my sister Susan said.

"That's too bad," I said. "Who's Jim?"

I was sitting at my desk in my office the following morning, and she, apparently, was sitting at *her* desk in *her* office. Although I could hear the tapping of keyboards in the background, it occurred to me that I had never, in all the years I had visited her in her up-to-date newsroom, actually seen her writing something. Of course television news writing consists of a maximum of television and a minimum of news writing—two or three lines a day are some guys' total output—but even so I would have expected to see her write *something* over the years.

"Jim Hilliard, silly," she said. "He's the lawyer who wrote you that highhanded letter."

"That highhanded letter on your behalf," I pointed out.

"Yes, well, he said to tell you that he's dreadfully sorry and would like to make it up to you."

"Tell him to hang loose and keep himself available. In my business I'm bound to need a lawyer someday."

"Actually," she said, "I think what he had in mind

was dinner. I'm not sure he's sorry an hour of his time's worth."

"An hour of his time costs more than dinner for two?"

"It would be dinner for three," she said. "And yes, I would say an hour in Jim's office with the meter running would cost more than dinner for five."

"The joke's on him. I'm a former jock. I'll eat as much as five."

"Fine," she said. "We'll pick you up at eight at your place. Wear a suit?"

"You mean eight *tonight?*" I said, but she had hung up already.

I had a fair idea of what dinner would be like. From the day I had first decided to become a private investigator, Susan had been after me to change vocations. It embarrassed her. She felt that mine was a disreputable, even dishonorable occupation, nearly as embarrassing as unemployment. She was, moreover, personally affronted that I had already experimented briefly with her own profession, journalism, and found it not to my taste.

My parents shared Susan's prejudice against my current line of work, although they didn't think too much of journalism, either. In Washington—and only in Washington—journalism is considered a respectable line of work, and lots of people in Washington have doubts about it, too.

My mother had always hoped I would be a lawyer, although I suspect she has reconciled herself to the impossibility of that by now. My father, on the other hand, had always wanted—expected—that I would play baseball, and he had never reconciled himself to the fact that *that* was not to be.

I had encouraged his fantasies, I suppose. Scouts came to see me from all over. They sat in the stands at my high school games, sometimes openly and sometimes (they imagined) surreptitiously. Later they would wander down to the locker room and talk with my coach. Then they started dropping by to talk to me. Eventually, one of them brought a contract, and eventually I signed it. Off I trotted to Florida for spring training. Who needs college when you can be rich at an early age? An ath-a-leet.

Within three years I was pitching Triple-A. I had an 18–6 record by Labor Day, and there was some talk that I might be called up to the Show to finish the season.

I never finished another game, never got past the fourth inning, in fact. With two out and two on I fired a pitch low and inside at a 200-hitting second baseman. The low-and-inside fast ball rose up to about letter height and drifted to the outside corner. The second baseman, knowing an early Christmas present when he saw one, pasted it over the centerfield fence.

The manager strolled casually out from the dugout, and I handed him the ball.

"Better luck next time," he said.

"I don't think so," I said.

I walked off the mound, through the dugout, and into the clubhouse. Without even changing clothes, I kept on walking to my car and drove home. I never went back.

At the age when my classmates were graduating

from college, I was finishing my career. I was a fast-baller without a fast ball and without anything to compensate for it.

And I didn't care. I was tired, and bored, and sick of three-hundred-mile bus trips, and Holiday Inns, and brown-grass outfields.

So I quit. I went back home to Washington where I had been born and raised. My father sulked, but my mother welcomed me like the prodigal returned. Surprisingly, so did Susan.

Susan, whom I barely knew. Ten years older than I was, already a rising star in local television news, beautiful, smarter than she ever permitted anyone to know about, she latched on to me and proceeded to remake my life. She launched a search for the perfect job and the perfect mate for her baby brother. She failed, of course, but it was fascinating while it lasted.

Despite the fact that I had neither experience nor college training, she prevailed on friends and colleagues and found a reporting job for me in a small newspaper bureau on Capitol Hill. The job didn't pay much, but it was supposed to be good training. I was surrounded by eager beavers, many of whom had Ivy League credentials, all of whom were heavily endowed with a sense of journalistic mission.

I lasted about a year and a half. I wasn't bad at it, I guess, but I just didn't care for it. My impression of journalism had been developed on Superman comic books and Little Theater revivals of *The Front Page,* where people ran around scooping other people and shouting "stop the presses." In real life, being a reporter was a lot like being an accountant or a bureaucrat, but at about half the pay. Washington journalism is intimately involved with digesting government reports, rewriting news releases, and attending press conferences. It was tedious, time-consuming, and—as nearly as I could determine—unrelated to anything real. I resigned.

"If it's glamor you want, let me get you a television job," Susan said. "As it happens, we have an opening right now."

"It isn't glamor I want," I said. "Baseball was glamorous."

"Television's a lot of fun."

"So was baseball," I said. "For a while. It didn't have anything to do with real life, either. Maybe I'll be a paramedic, or something."

"This is more exciting than real life," she said. "Washington is the capital of the world. You're not just writing news, you're writing history."

"Then it ought to be written by someone who doesn't keep nodding off during the most historic moments," I said. "Somebody else."

I signed on with a local detective agency and worked there until I could get my own license. I discovered that I liked the work. I don't think I was surprised.

After a while, when I felt ready, I borrowed some money from Susan, and others, and went into business for myself. Susan loaned me the money reluctantly, not because she couldn't afford to part with it—a successful television career and two successful ex-husbands had relieved her of most of the usual economic worries—but because she disapproved of my proposed uses for it. I promised to repay her with interest, and eventually she came through.

She continued, however, to express her disapproval through the traditional Big Sister avenues of expression: gentle needling, less-gentle needling, crude needling, malicious needling, unflattering remarks in public places, and occasionally, for variety's sake, sweet talk.

I didn't mind most of the time. I enjoyed Susan's company, despite everything, and I knew she meant well within the broad limits of that term as she would understand it. She felt that I was wasting my life and felt that she had a filial obligation to straighten me out. Her intentions were honorable, if misguided, and there were times when I wasn't sure she was wrong.

My father retired from his high-level government job, and he and my mother moved to Arizona. Susan was, in a sense, the only family I had left.

So now, with the telephone still warm in its cradle, I sat at my desk and considered my life or, as Susan would say, the shambles I had made of my life. At the age of 29 I was embarked on my third career. I had six hundred dollars in savings, a six-year-old car, a rented apartment, and some leftover pizza in the refrigerator. My net worth, including the pizza, was about two thousand dollars. On the other hand, my business was breaking even and threatening to turn a small profit if I didn't watch out, my reputation was more or less intact, I had a great secretary, and I could get Orioles games from Baltimore on my landlady's rooftop antenna. Besides that, my right arm hardly ever hurt anymore.

All things considered, things were developing nicely.

"Would you do me a favor?" I asked Georgie.

"Of course," she said, smiling.

"I'd appreciate it if you could line up an investigator for me in Rochester, New York. I need some information I can't get here." I gave her Eloise Leitner's name and address and told her about the newspaper advertisement I had found.

"You want to know what Mrs. Leitner has to say?"

"Right. Particularly, I want to know if she's ever seen a photograph of Irene and Harry Liston performing a death spiral. I think it may have gotten widespread publicity. Dumas had it hanging on the wall of his office the first time I was there."

She wrote that down. "What did Susan call you about?" she asked.

"Dinner," I said. "She wants me to meet her lawyer."

"The one who wants to take you to court?"

"Susan assures me that's all straightened out," I said. "We're all friends now, apparently."

"Think she's telling the truth?"

"I'll tell you after dinner when I find out who's picking up the check."

Georgie shook her head. "I like your sister a lot," she said. "But she's weird."

There was still no lime-green Volkswagen Rabbit parked at the skating rink when I returned that afternoon, and Dumas still wasn't around. Jane said she hadn't seen him all day, so I went to see Ray Martin, who seemed to be in charge in Dumas's absence.

"Jack?" he said, scratching his squared-off chin. "Haven't seen him at all today. Check his house?"

"He wasn't there, either."

"Can't help you then," he said. "He wasn't here when I arrived or when I came back for my second shift, and Jack and I don't exactly run in the same circles. I'll be on duty until eight tonight, though, and when I see him I'll tell him you're looking for him."

"Thanks," I said. I gave him one of my cards, which he studied at length before putting it away in his shirt pocket. I studied him while he read it. He had a long, thin face with high cheekbones, a slightly upturned nose, and watery blue eyes. His complexion was nearly as pale as his hair. It was the face of a man who spent a lot of time indoors.

He looked up and saw that I was watching him.

"I'll be sure to tell him," he said again.

"Right."

I had already started away when I remembered something I had meant to ask him.

"Do you have any idea what happened to the picture that was on the wall of Dumas's office yesterday?"

He turned away from me and began straightening the skates on the shelf behind him. "I don't remember what sort of pictures are on his wall," he said.

"There was only one," I said. "It was a black-and-white photograph of a couple of skaters in a death spiral. It was there yesterday, but it's gone now."

He shook his head. "I don't remember it," he said. "But we get a lot of pictures like that. Salesmen bring in a lot of them, and advance men for the ice shows sometimes stop by here with publicity shots. Some guys think they're nice pictures and hang them on the wall to brighten up the place. We've even got a couple hanging in the pro shop."

"Could I see them?"

He shrugged and opened the hinged section of the counter. He slipped out from behind it and led me to the shop, fumbling with his keys as we crossed the lobby.

He unlocked the door and slipped his hand inside to flip on the light. "Help yourself," he said. "I got work to do."

The pictures were the standard publicity photos you might expect to see in the newspaper before an ice show opens: young boys and girls frozen in mid-air, performing split jumps or posing in elaborate costumes and awkward positions on the ice. None of them was the picture I had seen before, and I returned to the rental counter and told Martin so.

"Maybe Jack took it home with him," he said. "There's no accounting for tastes."

"I don't think so," I said.

"Something interesting about this particular photograph?"

"I don't know," I said. "When I first saw it, I thought the girl in the picture was Debbie. Now I think it was Irene as a girl."

"Then maybe Jack *did* take it home," Martin said. "Jack's always had a thing for Irene."

"Maybe so," I said. But I knew I'd have seen it in his house, if it had been there.

* * *

There were still no lights on in the house on Euclid Place when I returned there that evening. I drove slowly past it in the half-light of dusk and looked for signs of life, but there were none. I looked for the yellow Toyota, but it wasn't in sight.

I parked about a half-block away and walked up and down the sidewalk in front of the house—once in each direction. The big bay window in front was curtained, and the shades were lowered.

After a while I climbed the high stoop and pushed the doorbell button. Chimes rang somewhere in the bowels of the house, but nothing else happened. I tried the doorknob, and it opened.

Just inside the door was a small foyer. Doors led off to the left and right, and a staircase in the center rose to the second floor. I opened the door on my left and entered a small parlor or sitting room with shabby, vaguely Victorian furnishings. A small credenza leaned against the far wall. A humidor and a collection of well-used pipes sat on one corner. I crossed the room and lifted the lid of the humidor, and the stale smell of tobacco arose.

Heavy-duty detection, McFarlin.

I crossed the hall and tried the door on the right. It opened into a room full of more old furniture, hulking in the gloom. In one chair, a high-backed wing chair, I could see what appeared to be the top of a head poking above the chair back.

"Anybody home?" I said. The person in the wing chair did not respond. I didn't blame him; I was trespassing in his house in the dark. I would probably be scared, too, under the circumstances.

"The door was open," I said. "So I just stepped inside."

Not quite true, of course. The door was unlocked, but not open.

He said nothing. I decided to take a chance and crossed the room to where he sat.

I once happened on a house where a man had recently put the barrel of a shotgun into his mouth and pulled the trigger. The aftermath of that particular death was, well, messy. By contrast, Jack Dumas sat quietly in the wing chair, staring into the middle distance, with only the small round red spot in his forehead to indicate that things were not as they should be.

"Whoa," I think I said.

His cheek was cold, and I didn't want to turn on the ceiling light to inspect the wound in greater detail.

I knew what I should have done, of course. There was a telephone on the table in the corner. I should have picked it up and called the police. Then I should have waited calmly until they arrived and explained how I happened to be in this house at this time in order to discover a corpse.

That was what I should have done. What I did was walk as casually as possible from the room, from the house, and to my car. I drove about a mile away and called the police anonymously. Then I cursed myself for my cowardice.

It occurred to me later that I had, at least, cleared up one question that had been bothering me. At least

I knew where Dumas had been hiding while I had been looking for him. He had been sitting quietly, waiting for me to find him, in a wing chair in the house on Euclid Place, NW.

Chapter Six

"**I**'ll have the prime rib," the lawyer named Jim Hilliard said.

He turned from the waiter, who was already sidling away, and wrapped a meaty hand around the frail stem of his martini glass. He took a long pull from the glass, and the pitted green olives in the bottom rolled and tumbled from the turbulence. I watched in fascination as one great, gray eyebrow arched, and then the other. He took in a mouthful of liquid and rolled it around in his mouth, swallowing it with an air of finality like a boa constrictor swallowing a small mammal. He set the glass down with precision, sighed elaborately, and looked at me directly for the first time that evening.

"So, Leo," he said. "May I call you Leo?"

"All right."

"So, Leo. Susan tells me you were a baseball player."

"Briefly."

"A pitcher."

"Yes."

"And now you're a . . . private eye."

"I prefer shamus," I said.

"And before that you were a journalist."

71

"Not a journalist. A reporter."

He cocked his eyebrow at me. "Is there some semantic distinction here that I don't understand?"

"I mean one of them does it, and the other one talks about it on television."

"It's just one of Leo's little jokes," Susan said.

"Very amusing," he said finally. My sister Susan employed her throaty chuckle for my benefit, or Hilliard's. Probably Hilliard's.

We were sitting in a restaurant on K Street. It was not French, or Szechuan, or upscale Italian like most of its neighbors. This was one of those power lunch places, where business-suited guys in their fifties came to engage in serious intimidation, and where they could still smoke cigars afterward. You could tell it was a power lunch place because it was named for the guy who owned it, and each table had a bowl of kosher dills the size of air-to-air missiles.

Restaurants are faddish things, and most places don't stay around long enough for me to learn their names, let alone eat in them. This place, however, was beyond fad. It had been in the same location for decades, virtually unchanged. They probably didn't have a single avocado in the house, and I'll bet they'd never had any kiwis, either.

I had been there once with my father, when he still liked me, and I had not been back. Nor was I likely to be back again after this. Private investigators rarely entertain clients, and clients never entertain private investigators. And if they were to begin doing so, it would be at McDonald's.

It was possible, of course, that I would be coming

again as Jim Hilliard's guest. A number of the men in Susan's life had bought meals for me over the years, apparently under the impression that I exercised some sort of influence over her. In truth, I had never met the man who exercised any appreciable influence over my sister, and I could think of no one less likely to do so than me. I ate the meals, anyway.

The practice had begun with her two eminently successful husbands, while they had still been her husbands, and had been extended to include most of the major contenders since then.

It was a crowded field. There had been the president of a Georgetown-based commercial real estate firm, who lost out because he was going bald. There was the owner of a Capitol Hill singles bar, who had proposed to her five times that she had told me about. There was a young Southern California congressman, a Republican of course, who had the dubious distinction of having been married more frequently than she had; she gave up on him because she felt he wasn't stable or mature enough for a lasting relationship. The most promising contender before Hilliard had been a small forward for the Washington Wizards. He had looked like a real comer for a while but had faded badly in the final quarter. I think he lacked the energy to keep up with her.

One of the local magazines publishes an annual feature on the ten most eligible women in Washington. Susan generally makes the list when she qualifies, which, I tell her, is usually in even-numbered years.

Compared to most of her choices, Hilliard seemed a reasonable alternative. He was close to her age—she

was thirty-eight and I put him in his early forties—
and financially successful. If he married Susan, he
would *have* to be successful. He was big but not fat,
and the deep tan he displayed even in December indicated that he didn't allow the pursuit of justice to
cut into inordinately into his leisure time.

Best of all, from my standpoint, he had not yet tried
to impress me with his importance. A Washington
man who can go thirty minutes without engaging in a
round of aggressive self-promotion is usually charac-
terized as "shy and retiring."

"Susan tells me you were a very good, er . . . reporter," Hilliard said. "Good instincts. An inquiring
mind."

"You've got to keep in mind that Susan's in television," I said. "In television, an inquiring mind is
someone who reads two newspapers."

"Has it occurred to you that you may have given
up a promising career in a respectable line of work
and replaced it with a dead-end job in a disreputable
field?"

"I prefer to think of myself as a small businessman,
the backbone of the American economy."

"How's your business doing?"

"Quite well, thank you," I said. "I'm paying my
bills."

"Oh, yes, you mean the letter I sent you. I have to
apologize for that. I'm afraid your sister gave me inaccurate information. I'm quite upset with her." He
favored her with a look composed more of affection
than of anger.

Susan smiled at me. "Isn't he marvelous?" she asked. "He isn't really angry at all."

"Ask me if I'm angry," I said.

"It's immaterial whether you're angry or not," she said. "I acted in your best interests. I'm just trying to get you out of that disgusting business and into something respectable."

"Is that your apology?"

"I have no intention of apologizing," she said, flushing a bit more than I would have expected. "The day will come when you'll thank me for what I've done."

The waiter appeared with our plates. I had ordered lamb, but the plate the waiter brought me contained a cut the size of a Shetland pony. Super lamb. I took a tentative bite, half expecting to encounter the flavor of horse. It tasted like lamb.

"What do you do when you're not detecting?" Hilliard asked. "Do you have you hobbies?"

"I paint some. I read some. I run some. I swim some. I get by."

"I see."

There was silence for a while as Hilliard worked on his meal. The prime rib flopped over the edge of his plate, and it looked great. Susan had ordered rockfish, and it looked very good. The wine came—something greenish and dry—and Hilliard gave it a judicious okay. We ate some more.

"Why did you quit the newspaper?" Hilliard asked finally, between mouthfuls.

"I was bored. And disgusted."

"Did you come to this conclusion slowly or did something precipitate your decision?"

I chewed a while and thought about whether I should bother trying to explain. Most people didn't care. I didn't care much anymore myself.

"Ever hear of the Brownsville Turnabout?" I asked.

"What is that A dance step?"

"A gimmick," I said. "I don't think they do it anymore. I don't even remember all the details, but basically it was a way to avoid some of the controls that we used to have on imported oil."

"How does this relate to the question I asked?"

"I'm coming to that. The way the controls worked in those days, you could import more oil from Mexico or Canada than you could from other countries—say, the Persian Gulf. The reason had to do with national defense, I think—Canada and Mexico were considered more stable allies, or something. At any rate, somebody found a way to get around this rule by bringing oil into the United States by sea at Brownsville, Texas. Then they trucked it under bond across the Rio Grande into Mexico. Once they got across the border, they just turned the trucks around and headed them back into the United States. Which made it Mexican oil instead of Arab oil."

"Very clever."

"Clever, yes, but basically dishonest. Mostly it was a game played by people who had no real interest in supplying oil to the United States, and they were aided by all those people who made the policies that created the loophole. Public policy wasn't the issue anymore. Making a profit wasn't even the issue—not the main issue. The main thing was playing the game, finding the loophole, outmaneuvering the opposition, putting something over on someone else."

"A debatable point," he said, "but I see what you're driving at. What I don't see is how this affected your decision to leave journalism."

"One day I had to cover a congressional hearing—a Senate hearing investigating the Brownsville Turnaround. It had all happened years before, of course, and it wasn't relevant anymore. The rules had changed again, and they were doing something else by then. But that's the kind of investigation the Senate does best."

"Also debatable," he said. "But go on."

"Well, in order to write about the investigation, I had to explain the Brownsville Turnaround. And I couldn't do it. I mean I understood what had happened, but I sat there at the typewriter and couldn't write it. It was a classic case of writer's block, but journalists don't have writer's block. They don't have time for it."

"So you gave up."

"I was in the Senate press gallery at the Capitol, and I just walked out and went home. A few weeks later they sent me a termination notice and a final paycheck, but by that time I was working for a detective agency and learning a new trade."

"It isn't exactly reputable work."

"Neither is working for a newspaper, most places. Washington's the only town in the country where it's considered respectable. I'm not sure that's an improvement."

"And you like this job better than the old one?"

"It's different."

"A bit sordid, though, don't you think? Prying into other people's personal lives, repossessing their automobiles, copying names off hotel registers."

"It's at least about something real," I said. "When I'm working for a client, I'm helping with a problem that affects him personally. It's about people—not con games and paper chases."

"Con games and paper chases," he said, musing. "Of course, con artists and paper chasers are people, too."

On my way out of the restaurant after dinner, I stopped and called my answering machine. It had recorded two calls: one from someone called Peter Blenheim in Rochester, New York, and one from Lieutenant Harold Barlow with the Metropolitan Police Department. I knew Barlow so I tried him first, but he wasn't in. I decided to try him and Blenheim later when I got home.

Hilliard was waiting with Susan in the lobby. Susan was wearing her full-length pearls, a gift from Husband Number One, who was the publisher of a string of newsletters for various segments of the oil and gas industry. Her blond hair spilled over the shoulders of her coat and looked even more lustrous than the pearls. Susan had received more than her normal allotment of both good looks and brains. In the decade that had intervened between her birth and mine, the formula had evidently been misplaced.

"You know," Hilliard said, when I joined them, "I think you're wasting your life. Journalism is an im-

portant career, and journalists contribute to our under-
standing of the world. What does a private investigator
contribute to society?"

"The same thing as most other people," I said. "The
taxable portion of his income."

He gave me an automatic, cocktail-party sort of
smile and turned away. "Are we all ready?" he asked
Susan. She nodded and took his arm.

"Care to join us?" he asked me. "We're just going
for a nightcap."

I shook my head. "Thanks, but no. I'm on a case,
and I have some things to do yet this evening."

"All right," he said. He turned to Susan. "Darling,
why don't you get us a taxi while I talk to Leo for a
moment?"

She hurried out into the night. A blast of cold air
hit me in the face as the door shut behind her.

"I have a confession to make, Leo," Hilliard said
after she had gone. "This dinner was your sister's idea,
not mine."

"I gathered that."

"She hoped that I could persuade you of the error
of your ways," he said. "Have I succeeded?"

"Not yet," I said.

He nodded. "I'm not sure I want to," he said. "There
are worse things to be than a private investigator."

"Thanks for the vote of confidence."

"Besides," he said, "I like you. I'd like to help.
Please feel free to come to me if you need legal advice
for any reason. Free of charge."

It was an overture of friendship, I supposed. I was
touched.

"Thank you, Jim. That means a lot to me."

"Possibly I can even steer some business in your direction if you prove to be good at your work," he said. "My firm handles quite a few criminal cases, and even some divorce work now and then."

"Well, thanks again," I said. "And I'll try to steer a little business your way, too. I handle quite a number of criminal cases myself."

I watched his eyes as he fought down the urge to take offense at my arrogance. After a struggle, he won out over the glitter in his eyes and gave me a weak grin, a quick handshake, and his back. Outside, through the glass door, I could see Susan easing into the back seat of a Diamond cab.

The sound that greeted my ears at six o'clock the following morning was not a gunshot, but it had the same emotional effect. It was the telephone. I groped for it in the darkness and heard a voice so cheerful it was almost offensive.

"Good morning, Leo. I'm so happy to have reached you. You're home so seldom."

"I tried to reach you last night, Lieutenant. You weren't in the office."

"I received your message. I'm sorry we missed each other yesterday. I've been looking forward to our little chat."

"What little chat?"

"Why, the little chat we're going to have this morning, Leo, as quickly as you can get here. And please don't call me Lieutenant; call me Harold. Friends shouldn't stand on formality."

"How about if I call you Handyman?" I asked.

"That would not be advisable."

I've often wondered what people who hear him first on the telephone are led to expect when they finally meet Lt. Harold "Handyman" Barlow in person: an aging preppie, perhaps, or an Etonian banished to the colonies. Whatever they expect, it is almost certainly not what they will get, which is a fiftyish, tall, rather heavyset black man who hails from Wilmington, North Carolina. As I lay in bed I could imagine him at his desk dressed, as usual, in a navy blue pinstripe three-piece suit, white-on-white shirt, and foulard tie, looking more like a lawyer than a homicide detective. In fact he had a law degree but was not a member of the bar, at least not the D.C. bar. He had acquired the nickname "Handyman" during the seventies, when he was on the narcotics squad, because of his reputed ability to discover evidence on suspected drug dealers.

"What do you want, Harold?" I asked.

"To talk, Leo. We have a great deal to discuss, you and I."

"You called me at six o'clock in the morning to make a luncheon date?"

"Well, actually, Leo, I was rather hoping to see you sooner than that. Almost immediately, in fact. Shall we say fifteen minutes?"

"Why?"

"There are any number of reasons, Leo, but perhaps one will suffice for the moment. I'm looking forward to hearing your explanation of how your fresh fingerprints wound up on the front door of a house that contains a recent corpse."

"What?"

He laughed. "Excellent. Just the right touch of surprise in your voice. Have you ever considered a career in the theater? You'd be good at it, I think."

"Lieutenant, I don't function well at six o'clock in the morning," I said. "Do you suppose you could knock off the bad Brit impressions for a while—at least until I could get down there to appreciate them in person?"

"You're asking me to deny my heritage, to turn my back on who I am. Surely you jest."

"You're no more English than I am."

"On the contrary, Leo, I am a great deal more English than you are. Your ancestors were Orangemen, I believe—Scotch-Irish extraction. When they were busy populating the Shenandoah hills, mine had long since emigrated from Nottinghamshire to North Carolina. There they had established tobacco plantations, and slave women who were also my ancestors."

"What about your African heritage?"

"Oh, that," he said. "Well, to tell you the truth I tried tracing my African heritage after Alex Haley published *Roots*, but it was a frustrating experience. Folks kept such poor records in those days, and I finally decided that it wasn't worth the trouble. After all, there was a perfectly serviceable English heritage available to me for no more than the price of a year's subscription to *Punch* and some paperback copies of Dickens. I *do* miss *Punch*."

I thought his heritage seemed to stem more from Monty Python than Charles Dickens, but I held my tongue.

"It wasn't easy, of course," he went on. "I had the devil's own time adjusting to the cuisine, if such it can be called. I still can't quite manage fish and chips, I'm afraid. But all in all, it was well worth the effort to seek my roots and find out who I am."

"Particularly if you can tick off some people along the way," I ventured.

"Indeed. That's not a sufficient reason unto itself, of course, but it's a more than adequate secondary factor," he said. "One of the best things about being an American is that sometimes one can pick one's ethnicity. I dare say that, if I wanted to do so, I could poke around the roots of my family tree and come up with a spot of Italian blood. Maybe I'll do so. It might be interesting."

"The food would be better, too," I said.

"But I didn't call you to discuss my lineage—or yours, either. You did say you would visit me, did you not? Shall we say, eight-thirty?"

"All right."

"Excellent. See you then."

After he had hung up—rung off, I suppose he would say—I called Irene Liston. I reached her at home before she left for the office and told her about everything that had happened, including my discovery of Jack Dumas's corpse.

"Who would want to kill poor Jack?" she asked.

"I don't know," I said. "Judging from Barlow's conversation, I'd say he doesn't know, either."

"What should I do?"

"I think you should keep Debbie away from the rink

for a few days," I said. "I need some time to look into things, and I can't do that while I'm guarding Debbie."

"All right," she said. "I'll keep her home today, at least. We can reconsider tomorrow."

"Thank you," I said. Then I hung up and dressed for my trip to Barlow's office.

Chapter Seven

"Let's try it again, shall we," said Lt. Harold "Handyman" Barlow.

"Must we?" I said.

"At five-thirty yesterday evening you went to a certain address on Euclid Place—the address you have given us—and knocked on the door."

"Approximately," I said.

"How can you approximately knock on a door?" Barlow said.

"Approximately five-thirty," I said. "I don't know the exact time. The clock on my dashboard said five-twenty-five when I got out of the car."

"Is the clock on your dashboard correct?"

"Frequently."

Barlow sighed. It was an immense, world-weary, monumental sigh, which he probably practiced each morning before the mirror.

"I am trying to persuade myself that you are co-operating with us, Leo," he said. "Do you suppose you could make it more convincing?"

There were five of us in the room: me, Barlow, Barlow's partner Alvin Geisele, and the framed portraits of the president and the mayor of the District of Columbia. Only two of us were smiling.

"I can only tell you what I know," I said. I smiled—that made three of us—and spread my hands. Barlow continued to frown. Geisele snorted and turned away.

"You knocked on the door at five-thirty," Barlow said again.

"Approximately."

"And what did you find when you went inside?"

"I found nothing," I said, "because I didn't go inside."

"Not even when you discovered that the door was unlocked?"

"Was it?"

Barlow cocked an eyebrow at me, studying me.

"Very well," he said. "You did not enter the house. What *did* you do?"

"We've been through all this before," I said. "All of it."

"And when you're finished, perhaps we'll go through it again."

I shrugged and attempted to look as nonchalant as I could. "I waited for someone to come to the door. When no one came, I decided the house was empty and I went away. I figured I'd come back some other time."

He slammed his hand on the desktop. I saw it coming, watched it descending, and I still jumped when it hit. The noise was deafening, like a shotgun at close range. Geisele was sitting on another desktop, and in my peripheral vision I could see him flinch slightly.

"Listen, Leo, I *know* you. You knocked on the door,

tried it, found it unlocked, and walked in. What I want to know—and it's *all* I want to know—is what you saw when you were there."

"I didn't see anything. I wasn't there."

"I'm not interested in yanking your license because of this petty little entry," Barlow said. "At least not yet. I'm after information."

And I should have given it to him. I should have owned up to my silly attempt to bend the rules and told him everything he wanted to know.

But I didn't.

In the first place, I didn't know anything—at least nothing that he didn't know already. I had spent considerable time thinking about what I had seen the night before, and I had concluded that my powers of observation must not be worth spit. I had vivid memories of the murder scene, but they were highly selective. I saw Jack Dumas's fixed stare. I saw the little round, red hole in his forehead. I felt the cold sweat breaking out on my own forehead. And that was it. I couldn't have described a single piece of furniture in the room aside from the wing chair Dumas was sitting in, or told Barlow whether Dumas had something in his hand, or whether the room was hot or cold. As an observer, I had drawn a blank.

In the second place, Barlow had annoyed me. I wasn't going to tell him anything because I didn't *want* to tell him anything. He hadn't been nice. He hadn't said please.

So for at least the twentieth time I said, "I didn't find anything because I didn't go inside."

Barlow reached across the desk and grabbed my

shirtfront. Then he lifted me slowly out of my chair and across the desk until my nose was only inches from his.

I marveled at the power in his arms. I felt like a bartender who had started mixing a martini and somehow set off a nuclear reaction by mistake. I wondered what were the odds of my getting in a punch before he flattened me. I decided they were too slim to contemplate.

But he didn't hit me. He stared into my eyes for a moment. Then, as carefully as if I were a china figurine, he placed me in my chair again. It was more frightening than if he *had* hit me, though less painful.

"Detective Giesele, please escort Mr. McFarlin from the building," he said with a sigh. I sighed, too.

"You got a real knack for ticking off the lieutenant," Geisele said in the stairwell.

"He started it," I said grumpily.

"You held up pretty good, though. I've seen him wilt guys just with words. Just melt them right down."

"Words don't scare me much," I said. "I spent a lot of time on Capitol Hill. They beat one another bloody with words, up there."

"We got other tools for that," Geisele said.

There was a pay phone downstairs, and I used it to call my office. It was about ten o'clock by that time.

"Where have you been?" Georgie asked. "I've been waiting for you."

"Visiting the Handyman," I said. "It wasn't very enlightening. Any calls?"

"I lined up an investigator in Rochester, like you asked. He's called twice. He said he called you last night but you never called back. I was beginning to worry."

"I had a busy night," I said. "Does the guy in Rochester have something for me?"

"He found Mrs. Leitner. She's in a nursing home, and she remembers Irene and Harry Liston very well. He thinks maybe you should talk to her yourself."

"I think so, too," I said. "Does he have an address?"

"He said to let him know when you're coming, and he'll meet your plane and take you there."

"I'll go on out to the airport and see what kind of flight I can get," I said.

"I'm one step ahead of you," she said. "You're booked on an eleven-thirty flight from National Airport. Your ticket is waiting for you at the ticket counter."

"Georgie," I said, "you're a wonderful person. If you weren't so impatient, you'd be perfect."

"What impatience? I'm a very patient person."

"Not patient enough. You rushed off and got married before you ever met me."

She laughed. "It's your own fault," she said. "You should have let me known you were out there." I hung up feeling flushed and tingly like an adolescent and also, because I knew and liked her husband, slightly guilty.

"Your name McFarlin?"

I turned to see a cop standing behind me.

"Yeah."

"Telephone," he said, pointing to a receiver at the

guard's desk. I picked it up and heard Handyman Barlow.

"I didn't want to discuss this in Detective Geisele's presence," Barlow said, "but I know you went inside the house. We found your fingerprint on a newel post. I hope you're not under the impression that you've put something over on me."

"Then why did you let me go?" I asked.

"I can't abide stupidity," he said. "And you were displaying more than your share. I concluded that you didn't know anything useful."

"An accurate conclusion."

"I reserve the right to change my mind about that, so I would recommend that you not take any trips for a while. I may want to talk to you again."

"I see."

"In the meantime, you might consider another line of work. I don't think you're suited to this one."

"I'll take it under advisement," I said.

"Do that. And remember what I said: don't leave town."

"Yes sir."

I hung up the phone and walked outside into a gray December morning, one of a continuing series. The cab that stopped for me didn't have a working heater, so it was very cold. I didn't mind. It was only a short ride to the airport, and it would be warm on the plane.

They gave me the last seat on the plane. It was in the middle of the row, in the front of the coach section, crammed into the space just behind the bulkhead. On the bulkhead was some sort of wall hanging done in various shades of orange, rust, and brown. It reminded me of someone's first, failed attempt at hooking a rug.

The aisle seat was occupied by a salesman of computer software catching up on his sleep. At the window was a white-haired woman whose glasses were hung by a thin gold chain around her neck. She was thin to the point of boniness, very neat, and her mouth was drawn into a tight line. She told me she had been in Washington for a demonstration against pollution.

As we neared Rochester, the plane banked sharply, and I could see Lake Ontario glinting in the sunlight. The lake was icing over, but under its surface I could see a blue-green finger jutting out toward the horizon.

"Kodak," said the woman at the window.

"Pardon?"

She pointed at the blue-green water. "Chemical waste," she said. "From the Kodak plant. Ruin the environment so the world can have color snapshots."

"Really? It just looks like shallow water to me."

She opened her slit of a mouth fractionally, then snapped it shut again and turned away to the window. She did not speak again.

A tall blond man stepped up to me as I came out of the airport concourse into the terminal.

"Leo McFarlin?"

"That's me."

"Pete Blenheim," he said. He extended a manicured hand that bore an onyx ring on the pinky.

"You picked me out easily enough," I said.

"I called your secretary and asked her to describe you. She said you were very distinguished looking."

"I must remember to give her a raise."

"She also said you were having trouble growing a beard and that you would not be wearing a suit."

"Oh."

"I'm parked out front," he said. "Unless it's been towed away."

He led the way, and I struggled to keep up. He was in his early forties, I guessed, with high cheekbones and deeply set green eyes. He had a height advantage of several inches on me and a reach advantage as well. His hands seemed to fall at about mid-thigh. It seemed to me that he would stand out in a crowd.

"Don't you have trouble blending in when you're tailing people?" I asked.

"Nope. I've got a technique for dealing with the problem."

"What's that?"

"I think invisible thoughts."

His burgundy-colored Ford Escort was parked right in front of the terminal door. I slipped into the passenger seat, and he slid, with difficulty, behind the wheel.

"This is my biggest problem on a tail," he said. "I'm a ten-gallon man in a five-gallon container."

It was midday by now, and traffic was light as we left the airport and entered the city. The first lunch-hour customers were beginning to filter into the fast-food restaurants along the street. We stopped at a McDonald's and picked up something to eat in the car on the way.

"The place we're going is a little north and east of here," he said. "Other side of town."

We passed through the center of the city and continued into the residential areas beyond it. After a while, I could see the blue horizon line of Lake Ontario ahead of us. We passed the sprawling Eastman Kodak complex on our left and continued until we reached a lakefront park. Then we veered to the right and kept going in an easterly direction. The houses changed gradually from modest bungalows to hillside mansions surrounded by hedges and thickets.

Blenheim turned off onto a street that wandered past a small strip shopping area with a mixture of drugstores, taverns, and dry cleaners. Red and green plastic garlands spanned the street and wrapped themselves like snakes around the lampposts. Red plastic candles spilled faint yellow puddles of light in the gray daylight, and shoppers jostled on the sidewalk.

After a few more blocks we turned off into a parking lot in front of a long, low wood-frame building. A gilt-and-plaster eagle hung over the door.

"This is it," Blenheim said, and shut off the ignition.

We sat a moment in the car and listened to the steel hood contracting in the cold. It sounded like metal popcorn. The sign on the pole in the parking lot said COLONIAL HAVEN REST HOME. The sign also bore an eagle on it, and the eagle was outlined in yellow neon tubing. The neon flickered and buzzed like an electric bug killer.

"Home sweet home," I said.

"Yeah."

The woman behind the desk was a fleshy bottle blond with huge thick eyeglasses that made her eyes appear to be twice normal size.

"It's Mr. Blenheim, isn't it?" she said brightly. "Here to see Mrs. Leitner again?"

"You remembered my name, Sadie. I'm flattered."

She smiled at him. "You can just go on back," she said. "You remember she's in room ten."

"I remember."

We walked together down the long corridor, and our shoes made faint sucking noises on the cheap linoleum. I felt the floor give when I stepped on it and rise with my foot when I lifted it. The gypsum-board walls were marred with the scuff marks of thousands of heels and medicine carts and serving trays.

"What kind of shape is Mrs. Leitner in?" I asked. "Is she coherent?"

"Depends on when you come, I think. I came to see her twice yesterday. Once she was, and once she wasn't."

He knocked softly on a half-open door, and a thin voice invited us in. A woman with hands like chicken feet sat propped up in bed, regarding us through half-lidded eyes.

"I know you from somewhere," she said to Blenheim.

"Peter Blenheim, ma'am," Blenheim said cheerfully to her. "I was here yesterday a couple of times. How are you today, Mrs. Leitner?"

"You're a detective," she said. "You asked me a lot of questions about Irene and Harry Liston."

"That's right," he said. "And I liked your answers so much I brought someone else to hear them. This is Mr. McFarlin."

She studied me intently. There was a half-sedated

look in her eyes, but there was a brightness there, too, like the reflective beads on a highway marker.

"Are you the one who's writing a book? I answered an advertisement in the paper."

"No ma'am," I said.

"Are you a detective, too? Like him?"

"Yes ma'am."

I handed her one of my cards, and she snatched it from me and held it close to her face. Then she handed it back.

"You don't look like a detective," she said. "You look like a hippie."

"A good detective shouldn't look like a detective," I said.

She snorted in amusement. Her bobbed red hair, now turning pink as the gray overtook it, bounced on her head.

"What do you want to know?" she asked, and settled back against her pillow.

"Everything you were prepared to tell the man who placed the newspaper advertisement," I said. "Tell me about Irene and Harry."

"He didn't answer my letter."

"Imagine that he did," I said. "Suppose he asked you to tell him about Irene and Harry. What would you say?"

The glittering eyes softened for the first time. "Oh, they were good," she said. "The best I ever had."

"Champions."

"Potential champions," she said. "I could see that. Harry was strong, and Irene was beautiful, and their poise and presence were almost perfect. And they had good form. They had a death spiral that would break your heart."

I had a fleeting vision of another death spiral—the one that ended with Debbie Liston sprawled unconscious on the ice.

"How did you become Harry and Irene's coach?"

"Accident," she said. "Irene's mother brought them around one day. They had been taking lessons at another ice rink that was not, well, as good as some. Their instruction had been . . . flawed. I almost didn't take them."

"Why not?"

"I was busy. My son was working very hard on his own training. I didn't really want another pupil, least of all a pair of them."

"What changed your mind?"

"I auditioned them," she said. "I had them skate around the rink a few times, just steady stroking so I could see how well they had picked up the fundamentals, and they were passable on the basics. A lot of teachers don't work their pupils very hard on things like stroking, edges, and body position. I could see that they would never make it individually, but they seemed to work well together. So I asked them to show me their program."

"They had a routine already worked up?"

"Oh, yes. They had been in some club-level competitions around the area. I knew that."

She shifted uncomfortably in her bed. "Am I telling you what I want to know?"

"I don't know."

"When will you know?"

"I don't know that, either. Maybe when I hear it."
She nodded.

"They performed for you," I prompted.

"Yes. And I could see that Irene's mother had recognized the spark of true talent when she had seen it. The irony, of course, is that her primary interest was Irene, but it was Harry who had the most ability."

"Irene was a hanger-on?"

"Oh, no. Neither of them would have been successful alone. Harry had the strength, but he needed Irene to set him off. They were only ten then—in fact, Irene was eight—but already you could see that she would be a beautiful woman who would hold the audience's attention. And she skated well enough, though not as well as Harry. And she had determination, which was something Harry lacked."

"He didn't try hard enough?"

"He was a natural skater. He told me once that he had skated the first time he had set foot on the ice, and by the end of his first week he was performing jumps and attempting a spin. He didn't have to work very hard. I don't think he cared very much."

"Why did they quit skating?" I asked. I had already heard the story from Irene, but I thought there might be some interesting discrepancies in hearing it from another source.

There were.

"It was Harry's idea," she said. "They got married, and afterward they had a tough time financially. Harry was impatient. He wanted better things. He wanted money."

This didn't sound like the story I had heard from Irene.

"I gather he didn't turn professional," I said.

"No," she said. "He did a stupid thing. He robbed a liquor store."

Chapter Eight

"I don't understand," I said.

"Harry Liston was a fool," Eloise Leitner said. "He went into a liquor store over in Brighton and shot and killed the poor old man who was on duty that night. He got about a thousand dollars."

"And then he was shot by police?"

"Oh, no. He got away. He wore a Halloween mask, and it was a couple of days before the police were able to piece together enough information to trace it back to Harry."

"How did they do that?"

"Somebody got a license number," Blenheim said. "I checked it out with the police. Harry had used his mother's car. At first, she said it had been stolen, but they came to the conclusion that Harry had borrowed it."

"They found some of the money in Harry's room, later," Mrs. Leitner said.

"Harry's car skidded on an oily patch in the road a few days later," Blenheim said. "They found it smashed into a bridge abutment with Harry's body inside. The car had caught fire, and the body was unrecognizable. This is all in the report I'm sending you."

"How did they know it was Harry's body?"

Blenheim shrugged. "Right size, right coloring, his car. And then they had his father's identification."

"His father lived in the area?"

"No, but he happened to be in town at the time, and he agreed to come view the body."

The bird woman looked at me suspiciously. "That's what you're really interested in," she said. "The robbery. You don't care about Irene and Harry."

"Mrs. Leitner, believe me," I said. "This is the first I've ever heard about a robbery."

I wasn't sure what, if anything, it meant, but it was an interesting piece of information. It probably *did* mean something—fit into the overall fabric somehow— but I couldn't see the connection.

"Where's Harry's father now?" I asked. "Still living?"

"I don't know," she said. "Harry's father and mother were divorced long before I began to teach the children. I never met him, but I understand that he moved away soon after he separated from his wife."

"And the mother?"

"She died," Mrs. Leitner said. "She had cancer, and it sneaked up quickly. It must be six years ago, now."

We talked for a while after that, but I gained no information of value. I came away with the impression that Eloise Leitner confined her interest to a limited number of subjects and a limited number of people. Irene and Harry had made the cut, but their parents, relatives, and siblings had not. Neither, apparently, had I.

I thanked her finally, and Blenheim and I turned to leave the room. A thought struck me.

"Do you remember a photograph of Irene and Harry performing a death spiral?" I asked. "It may have been published somewhere. The one I saw looked like a professional job." I described it to her as well as I could.

"I believe there *was* a photograph like that," she said. "It was published in the local paper and reprinted in several others, I think. It was a good picture, and it captured their style. The photographer made a copy of it for me."

"Do you still have it? I'm trying to locate it. I'd be happy to copy it and return it to you."

She shook her head. "Oh, I lost it years ago," she said. "It may have been in my house somewhere, but I sold the house and all the furnishings when I moved in here."

"When was that?"

"Last year, I think. Or was it two? I can't keep up with time the way I used to."

Another dead end. I stood up and made ready to leave her. "Thank you for your time, Mrs. Leitner," I said.

"Time," she said. "It's the cheapest thing I own. I don't have much left, but what I have goes begging."

A man appeared in the doorway. He was short and round, with brown hair that clung in tight curls to his head like the ringlets on a Roman sculpture. The green eyes flicked quickly from me to Blenheim to Mrs. Leitner.

"I'm sorry, Mother," he said. "I didn't realize you had company. I'll come back later."

"You, Teddy, come back here," she said. "I see little enough of you in this awful place without your disappearing on me now. These gentlemen are just leaving, so you get back in here and *visit*."

Teddy smiled ruefully at us and slipped into the room as Blenheim and I slipped out.

"Are all your cases like this one?" Blenheim asked.

"No, sometimes it's just your routine counterespionage stuff. You know, microdots and cyanide tablets and things like that."

"Well, it's more interesting than the stuff I've been doing," he said. "A lot of it is repo work, which is just one or two steps removed from carjacking, if you ask me. These days I don't even get any interesting divorce cases."

"I don't like divorce cases," I said. "I try not to handle them. But I'd think there'd be a lot of business in divorces."

He shook his head. "To get divorced, you first gotta get married."

We had just reached the car when Teddy came out of the building behind us.

"Mother told me you were asking about Irene and Harry," he said. "That's a long time ago."

"That's right," I said. "Is there anything you can tell me?"

"I don't know," he said. "But I knew them both. Is Irene in some kind of trouble?"

"What makes you think that?"

"Mother said you were a detective," he said. "Most people don't have detectives asking about them."

"Irene hired me to look after her daughter," I said. "Along the way I stumbled onto something that seemed to point back here. I don't know what it's about, but I don't think she's in any trouble."

"I'm glad to hear it," he said. "She was a good kid, Irene."

"What about Harry?"

"Harry." He made a face. "Did you ever see an athlete who had everything—natural style and an intuitive sense of what to do—who threw it all away? That was Harry. He wanted everything, and he wanted it yesterday, and he wouldn't settle for anything less. So instead of becoming a world-class skater he became a murderer and an armed robber. Harry was a bum."

"Sounds like you knew him well."

"I was best man at the wedding," he said. "Not by choice, but they needed somebody. Mother assigned me."

"What did your mother have to do with it?"

He laughed a metallic sort of laugh. "She had everything to do with it. Mother's the one who pushed them to get married. Harry never wanted it. I suppose Irene wanted it, but Irene wanted anything that looked good. And Harry always looked good."

"Why would your mother care whether they were married?"

"It made all the difference to her," he said. "Apart, Irene and Harry were just two teenagers with more hormones than sense. Married, they were the love children, the darlings of the old ladies and adolescent girls who read those drippy romance novels. A lot of those people go to skating competitions."

"I thought Irene's pregnancy ruined their skating careers." I remembered that Irene had said as much.

"Who knows? If you're an amateur, well, who knows what the amateur judges would have done back then if they were faced with a shotgun marriage. But in the pros, heck, they would have been more valuable than ever. The ice show publicity flacks would have loved it."

"I guess I'll never understand this sport," I said.

"It isn't a sport," he said. "You gotta be in good shape to do it, and you gotta have skill to do it, but it isn't a sport. It's more like ballet. A ballet dancer's got to be a good athlete, but nobody ever called him a sportsman."

"So what is it?"

"It's a business, that's all. A branch of the entertainment business, I guess, and you can make a lot of money in it. But it ain't a sport. The judges know who they want to win before they even open the doors."

"I see," I said. "Well, thank you for your help, Mr. Leitner."

"Call me Charles," he said.

"Not Theodore?"

"That's a nickname she gave me," he said. "As a child. Always chubby like a teddy bear. I never could shake it."

He took my hand and pumped it, and he handed me a business card. It said he was a stockbroker, but I didn't have the impression he was a very successful one. "If you need anything else," he said, "just call me. Maybe I'll remember something that can help you. I don't know exactly what you're looking for, but I'll try to help."

"I don't know what I'm looking for, either," I said. "But if I find out, I'll call you."

"I gather you used to be a skater yourself," I said. "Why did you give it up?"

"I didn't want to be a figure skater," he said. "I wanted to play hockey. Mother's never quite forgiven me for making a failure out of her."

He turned to go back inside.

"Where can I find Harry's father?" I asked.

"I don't know. I never met the man. I guess he moved away before I ever met Harry."

"But he was in town when Harry was killed."

"I know. Just coincidence, I guess. They say he left town again after identifying the body."

"I see. Well, thanks, anyway."

He smiled grimly and returned to the nursing home. Blenheim and I got back in his car and drove away in the direction of the airport. The sun was sinking low in the sky by this time, creating long fingerlike shadows of the bare trees. The light flickered as we drove through the shadows, like a silent movie. It interfered with my thinking, and it depressed me, too.

"There's something else you could do for me," I said to Blenheim. "How about checking out that robbery that Harry Liston was supposed to be involved in? I'd like to know more about the circumstances."

"Why don't you ask your client?"

"I will," I said. "But I have a feeling I won't learn much. I don't think she's telling me everything."

"You mean she's lying to you?"

"Maybe. Maybe she just doesn't like bad memories."

"In our business," Blenheim said, "pleasant memories aren't much help."

We pulled up in front of the terminal building. As I got out, he reached across the front seat and shook my hand.

"I'll get back to you in a day or two. If you're ever back this way, give me a call. It's a pleasure doing business with you."

"Thanks."

"Was it a worthwhile trip?" he asked. "Did you find out what you wanted to know?"

"I think I did," I said. "I'm just not sure if I know what it was."

He nodded as if that made all the sense in the world. I got out of the car. The burgundy Escort moved away in the dusk. I went inside the terminal, where it was warm and bright, and looked for a telephone and a reasonable chair, in that order.

In the terminal I got a handful of change at the newsstand and called Jane Borman at the ice rink, long distance. A young male voice, obviously one of Dumas's "merit scholars," answered the phone.

"She's on the ice right now, and I'm not permitted to interrupt a class session," he said. "I'll take a message, though, and she can call you back."

"She can't call me back," I said. "I'm in the airport, and they're calling my flight."

"Where are you going?"

"I'm not going, I'm coming. I'm in Rochester, New York, and I'm flying back down to Washington tonight. I need to talk to her when I get there."

"Right. Let me get a pencil."

"Ask her to stick around the rink and wait for me, will you? I'll stop off to see her when my flight gets in."

I could hear him scribbling. "When's your flight get in?"

"Nine-thirty."

"We're upper Connecticut Avenue. If you're coming into National Airport, and you take the Rock Creek Parkway, you ought to be here by ten."

"It'll be later than that," I said. "My car's at my apartment. I'll take the subway to my apartment, pick up the car, and then drive up there. Figure more like ten-thirty."

"Okay. Where's your apartment?"

"Foggy Bottom. Twenty-third Street."

"Right. I'll give her the message."

To most Washingtonians, Rock Creek Park is just something you drive through, or jog through, or run through, on your way to the Maryland suburbs. You don't find it listed in the tourist guidebooks, though you do find it on the maps because it's too large to ignore. It's a long, narrow, wooded ravine, through which flows a pleasant, polluted stream that begins above the fall line in Maryland and empties into the Potomac.

A network of black-topped roads winds through the ravine, under high-arched stone viaducts and among massive oaks and hemlocks. The trees appear to have been there since the last dinosaur sank into the muck. In fact, Rock Creek Park is nearly all second-growth forest. It was pretty much cleared by the first settlers, and few of the existing trees are more than 150 years old.

I entered the parkway from Virginia Avenue just above the Kennedy Center. There was little traffic.

I wished I were home in bed. I was tired, and my mind wandered. Just below Cathedral Avenue, in fact, I found myself suddenly in the wrong lane. I was driving in the left-hand lane when I discovered, with a jolt, that I needed to be in the right-hand lane instead.

It was too late to make the lane change legally; a snow-covered median strip with a high curbstone stood in the way. Since there was no traffic immediately behind me, however, I pulled over and stopped. I sat there for a moment, deciding what to do.

In my rearview mirror I could see that the only other car on the road had also stopped. He was about fifty yards behind me. He had probably made the same mistake I had—a common enough error because the parkway wasn't well marked. Or else he was having engine trouble.

I slipped into reverse and backed up until I could switch lanes without driving over the median divider. Then I moved to the other lane and started off again.

In my mirror I saw the car behind me had also

switched lanes. I had at least prevented him from making the same mistake that I had made.

I passed the rear entrance of the National Zoo, and the road began to narrow considerably. It was now two lanes, undivided, and the speed limit had dropped from forty-five to twenty-five miles an hour. The shoulder had virtually disappeared, and the dry snow along the roadside drifted over the roadway itself. I could feel my tires slipping a bit as I drove along. I slowed down.

Beyond the zoo I entered a close little tunnel, lit by a bank of fluorescent lights so bright that my headlights became superfluous for a while. As I emerged from the tunnel I could see the car behind me entering it. It was a large blue General Motors car—possibly a Pontiac—with a cream-colored vinyl top.

Beyond the tunnel the road narrowed still further as it tracked the path of the creek bed. There was a thin layer of ice over the creek, and every few yards my headlights would pick up a gaping hole where the ice had broken through. Oak and hickory lined the roadside, their thick branches laden with phosphorescent snow.

The car behind me was now closing the gap between us rather rapidly, as if the driver was intending to pass. That, of course, was absurd; the road was too narrow, the speed limit was too low, and there were too many ice patches on the blacktop.

When he got to within a couple of car lengths, he switched his headlights to high beam. I reached up to adjust my mirror and heard the sound of glass shattering. A small round hole appeared in the windshield near my hand.

It took me a second or two to recognize the hole for what it was, and by that time another had appeared alongside it. The new hole was farther away on the passenger side of the windshield. He was using a handgun of some sort. He'd have to be lucky to hit me from a moving automobile.

Still, there was no point in making it easy for him. I stepped hard on the accelerator, and my tires spun, bit into the pavement, and shot the car forward.

The car behind me dropped back for a moment, but the driver soon recovered and began regaining ground. It was a faster car than mine. Most cars were faster than mine.

I glanced at the holes in the windshield. They were small calibre, perfectly round. Tiny shards of safety glass spread across the dashboard, and I could see additional fragments blowing around on the hood of my car. The rear window had also broken into fragments where the bullets had entered the car.

He was out of range for the moment, but he was closing fast. The road was too narrow for fancy maneuvering. My best bet was to get out of the park and onto the well-lit, populated streets of the city above me, where the sound of gunfire might attract attention.

I glanced at my speedometer, which was a mistake. When I looked away from the road, my right front wheel scrubbed the curb, and I had to wrench it back on the road. The speedometer needle was hovering around seventy.

Ahead of me on the left, a drive led into a combination parking lot and turnaround loop. I saw it too late. As I frantically wrestled the steering wheel to make the turn, the car drifted into a sideslipping skid. It slid diagonally across the road and slammed hard against a steel lamppost. I felt myself being flung violently against my shoulder harness, and the red lights on my dashboard lit up all at once.

The Pontiac had similar problems. The driver hit the brakes, probably when he saw me trying to turn around, and we narrowly avoided colliding. Then he skidded about fifty yards off the road on the right-hand side and came to rest with the car's nose in a snow bank. I could see taillights glowing and hear the labored groan of his starter motor.

I tried to start my own car, but the engine wouldn't catch. I could hear it trying to turn over but not quite making it. My battery was getting weaker, and the lights on my dashboard were getting dimmer.

I switched off the ignition and took a deep breath. Whenever I had gotten in a jam I had a deep-breathing exercise that used to help calm me down. I tried it now, and it helped a little.

The driver's side door opened on the Pontiac, and a man got out. He was wearing a sheepskin-lined jacket with fleece spreading out onto big lapels in front. He wore gloves. He carried something small, black, and lethal in his right hand.

I flipped the ignition again, but the starter responded with something less than enthusiasm. In my mirror I saw the man close the door of the Pontiac and begin walking in my direction, casually, gun at his side, taking his time.

My engine was trying to catch hold, but the cold

weather had taken its toll. It was laboring hard, but it just couldn't quite turn over. Why not?

He was about thirty yards away now, and closing. I considered abandoning the car and taking to the woods, but I discarded the idea. If he shot me in my own car, he would have to dispose of my body somehow—a minor problem, certainly, but a problem nevertheless. In the woods, he could simply shoot me and walk away.

I could see the outline of his face in the glow of my taillights. It was a long, angular face, and I thought I had seen it before, but the light was poor. I couldn't be certain.

He was almost in pistol range now. Why didn't he shoot? He still held the gun at his side.

It occurred to me suddenly that my lights were still on, draining the battery. I switched them off, and the darkness closed in.

I lost sight of him in the darkness for a moment. When I could see him again I realized, with a shock, that he hadn't moved. Maybe he thought I had a gun, too. I didn't, but I suddenly wished that I had one.

But he didn't know I was unarmed, and maybe that would give me an extra second or two. I used as many as possible in order to rest my car's battery. Then I tried again to start the engine.

The starter motor groaned and croaked for a sickening moment, and the engine roared to life. The car rolled forward until the bumper jostled a chain stretched across the driveway in front of me.

Wrong direction. I was going to have back up—in the direction of the man with the gun.

In that case, I thought, I had better make this unpleasant necessity into a virtue. I jammed the shift lever in reverse, squirmed down in my seat, and stepped hard on the accelerator. The car spurted backward, eating up the distance between us.

Through the rear window I could see the man rooted in one spot, and I thought his jaw dropped. He moved into a crouch, steadying the gun with both hands, the stubby barrel pointed right at me.

I flipped on my lights again, illuminating him in the taillights, and aimed the car at him. He hesitated for a moment, which was a mistake. He was using up the brief time left for getting off a shot before diving out of my way.

I heard the bullet thunk into the steel of the trunk. Then he was diving into a low-lying snowbank and rolling down behind it.

I was on the pavement. Quickly I shifted to DRIVE and floored the accelerator. The tires spun on the pavement, and we shot forward.

The man with the gun still lay on his back at the side of the road. As I sped off I could see him pick himself up and spring for his own car. No matter. I had a lead on him now, and I wouldn't let him catch me. And he might not be able to get his car started, jammed in the snow bank as it was.

He didn't catch me. About a quarter of a mile farther I found a road that led upward, out of the park toward Connecticut Avenue. By now the bullet holes in my windshield had developed into cracks, which radiated out like the fine tracings of a spiderweb. It was getting nearly impossible to see where I was going.

I found a shopping center parking lot and left the car inconspicuously in the middle of a number of others. I found a pay telephone nearby and made several calls.

As it happened, Handyman Barlow wasn't in his office, and no, they didn't know where I could reach him. Or when. Would I like to leave a message? I would, and did.

Jane hadn't gotten my message, so she wasn't upset that I was late. I told her it would be another thirty minutes before I could get there. She said that would be fine.

There were no calls on my answering machine.

That left Irene Liston. She was at home, and she answered on the first ring. I explained what had happened.

"Did you see who shot at you?" she asked.

"Fleetingly. Average height, long face. He was wearing a dark stocking cap and a sheepskin jacket."

"It doesn't sound like anyone I know. Would you recognize him again?"

"Maybe," I said. "Maybe not. But that's not why I called. I think you should reconsider your decision to let Debbie continue skating."

"Because someone fired at you tonight? You don't know that this is related to Debbie."

"Mrs. Liston, my life isn't that exotic. People don't shoot at me. I don't go into crack houses. I watch people, look through public records, and ask questions. Nothing I'm doing right now involves guns or death in any way—except your case. Believe me, this is re-lated somehow."

There was a long silence.

"I'll reconsider," she said finally.

Chapter Nine

Over the door of the ice rink was a hand-lettered poster that read: *We are starting a memorial fund in memory of Jack Dumas. Contributions gratefully accepted. See Janice in the box office.*

Below the message was a crude drawing of a pair of figure skates and the name "*Columbia Blades Figure Skating Club.*"

Janice turned out to be a pleasant thirtyish woman with braces on her teeth and a faint aroma of cloves about her. She said the sign had gone up only a few hours earlier, but there had already been a few small contributions.

"Jack's death was on television tonight," she said. "On the six o'clock news. As soon as I heard about it, I pulled out this sheet of poster board and made the sign. I have poster board around the house all the time because the kids are always needing it for school."

"What did the news report say?"

"Oh, they talked to a lot of the regular skaters here, and they all said what a wonderful man he was. Easygoing. There were television crews just swarming all over here earlier in the evening."

"Did the news report say how he died?"

"They said he'd been shot to death in somebody's house. Not his own, apparently. A house in the District. I don't think the police know what he was doing there."

"Jack hadn't been working here very long, had he?" I asked. "Three or four months or so?"

"Oh, it's been longer than that," she said. "It would have been a year in January. I remember because it was just before the end of the school semester. He worked into the routine quickly."

Inside, the rink was teeming with skaters of assorted sizes and ages. Jane was still on the ice, talking earnestly with a middle-aged woman in a skating dress of cerulean blue. The dress emphasized her thighs, which did not benefit from the attention. Beside her, Jane was dressed in jeans, a blue parka, and heavy, brightly colored mittens. She looked great. As she talked, she slipped fluidly into an arabesque and glided backward in a small circle at center ice. The woman watched carefully, and in a moment she attempted a wobbly version of the same movement.

I watched them from behind the glass. After a moment Jane saw me there, smiled, and mouthed the words, "five minutes." She held up five fingers for emphasis. Her student noticed the gesture, and she beamed at me the way onlookers smile at couples in the park. I could do worse, I thought, than be coupled with Jane Borman.

In the lobby, a teenage boy commanded the rental counter. He was holding court for a gaggle of adolescent girls in short skirts and knitted leggings. I caught his eye, and eventually he disengaged himself and sauntered in my direction.

"Need skates?"

I shook my head. "Just looking for Ray Martin."

"He left about an hour and a half ago."

"Will he be in tomorrow night?"

"Hard to say," the boy said. "He doesn't usually work nights. He might *start* working nights, now that Mr. Dumas is dead."

"Is Ray the assistant manager?"

"Ray? Uh, no. He's just another grunt, like me. He looks distinguished, with that gray hair and all, but he's just a part-timer."

"Where could I reach him now, if I had to?"

"I don't know where he lives. Mr. Seagram would know, but he's gone home."

"Who's Mr. Seagram?"

"He's the owner. He doesn't normally get involved in operations, but he's had to come around since Mr. Dumas died."

"Where can I reach Seagram?"

"He's in the phone book, but he's not home tonight. I remember he said something about a dinner date."

"What's his first name, in case I want to look him up?"

"Arthur," he said. "But if you can wait until to-morrow, he'll be here in the morning."

Out on the ice, Jane had finished her lesson. I met her at the entrance.

"Have time to help out your friendly neighborhood private eye?" I asked her.

"That depends," she said. "Does the private eye have time for dinner? I'm starved."

"Haven't you eaten yet? It's ten o'clock."

"I had breakfast. But that was about four-thirty this morning."

"No lunch?"

"No time."

She sat before a locker and began unlacing her left skate boot. "I started at five o'clock this morning, and I worked through without a break. I had my skates off once, when the Zamboni broke down during resurfacing. That was about thirty minutes."

"I couldn't survive a schedule like that," I said.

"You could if you wanted to," she said. "But *only* if you wanted to."

Outside, the wind was cold, and the air was damp. Overhead, the low-hanging clouds reflected the light from downtown, staining the sky a bright reddish-violet color. There was probably more snow in those clouds, and we had already had more than our share for so early in the season. It made me shiver just thinking about it.

"Your car or mine?" she asked brightly.

"It'll have to be yours," I said. "Mine is a little under the weather."

I pointed to it in the parking lot. The windshield was cobwebbed now with hairline fissures. She peered at it in the darkness and whistled softly.

"Did you have an accident?" she said. "The roads are slippery tonight."

"It was no accident," I said.

Her car was a chromium yellow Porsche, which was

sitting in solitary splendor in an out-of-the-way location as if it were too good to sit alongside the mixture of Hondas and Oldsmobiles that populated the parking lot. It was.

"Wow," I said.

"I know," she said, smiling. "It's my pride. My only luxury. I don't drink, and I don't have television. My apartment is furnished in Early Cardtable. I can't really afford a Porsche, but it's my only indulgence."

"I like your sense of priorities," I said. "Will you marry me?"

She laughed it off. "Would you like to drive? I'm dog-tired, and I'd be happy for someone else to be the chauffeur."

"You'd let me drive this beautiful machine even after seeing the mess my car is in?"

"That wasn't your fault," she said. "If it were, there'd be more damage to your front end. That wasn't caused by a collision."

"Thanks for the confidence."

I slipped into the driver's seat and switched on the ignition as she got in the other side. The car burst into life, and I eased out on the clutch.

"I thought ice skaters made a lot of money," I said.

The car rolled forward. I had meant for it to roll backward.

"I think you're in the wrong gear," she said. "Headliners with the ice shows make pretty good money. I was in a show for a while, though not as a star. The money was okay."

"Why did you quit?" I asked. The car shuddered

and stalled. I decided I was still in the wrong gear—not first anymore, but not reverse, either.

"I got tired," she said. "It's nine months on the road, sometimes a new city every night, living in hotels, eating out for every meal. I think you're in third gear now."

"Sorry."

"It's okay. Foreign transmissions are hard to get used to, at first."

"I mostly drive automatics," I said.

"Well, there you are then. At any rate, I had enough of it after a year. Some girls don't last even that long. There's a lot of turnover. No, that's second gear."

The shift lever slipped easily into position this time. I eased out on the clutch and applied a feathery touch to the accelerator pedal. I'd heard about the power these cars had, but I didn't feel it. The engine raced, but the car remained stationary.

"I think you're in neutral now," she said.

"Uh-oh."

"Why don't I drive?" she said. "I'm more familiar with it."

"I'll get the hang of it."

"I'm sure you will," she said. "But in the interest of time."

"But you said you were too tired."

"I've gotten my second wind now," she said. "I feel fine. Really."

"You've had a long day."

"I haven't been out of town, like you. It's no trouble, really. Just slide over the shift lever, and I'll go around and get in the other side."

"But . . ."

"Really, it's no trouble."

I slid over, and she got in on the driver's side. She slipped the car into reverse and eased out of the parking space. The car responded like a well-bred mare. It oozed into the Connecticut Avenue traffic as if it were coated with oil. I fought back the urge to sulk.

"Mind if I ask *you* a question?" she said.

"Go ahead."

"Is there a college somewhere that offers a course in private detecting?"

"There may be, but I didn't attend it," I said. "I didn't go to college. I apprenticed at an agency here in town. Then when I had my license, I decided to go out on my own."

"Why didn't you go to college?" she asked. "You seem bright enough."

"Lack of interest, mostly. I thought I had a career that didn't require a college degree."

"You mean private detecting?"

"That came later. First, I spent three years pitching in the minor leagues. Then when I gave that up, I got a reporting job in a news bureau here for a while. This is career number three."

"Were you a good pitcher?"

"For as long as I lasted, but then my arm gave out. I could probably still pitch a couple of good innings, but I wouldn't be able to tie my shoes the next day."

She nodded knowingly. "With skaters, it's the knees that go first," she said.

"Football players, too."

"So I've heard," she said. "Do you miss baseball?"

"No. By the time I'd turned pro I was already getting tired of it. I'd pitched in Little League, Babe Ruth, American Legion, and during the off season I used to practice by throwing rocks and snowballs. After a while, pitching was just something I did that hurt a lot. I don't even go to games much anymore."

"You were pretty dedicated for someone who didn't like what you were doing," she said.

"I liked it when I started," I said. "You're looked up to by other kids, especially the girls, and you're always chosen first when they're making up teams. Even when I didn't like it anymore. I didn't think I could quit. My father is a baseball nut, and I didn't have the courage to face him and tell him the truth."

"Maybe you hurt him more by staying with something you didn't like, just to please him."

"That's what I told myself when I decided to quit," I said. "But the next time I saw him, I learned better. He called me a quitter, among other things."

"Surely he doesn't still hold a grudge."

"He tries not to, but he can't help it. He thinks I'm malingering. He thinks I could still pitch if I wanted to."

"That's a cruel way to be."

"No, he's right. If I wanted to pitch bad enough, no amount of pain would stop me."

"Are you angry with him?"

"I don't know," I said. "I don't want to be. He's just a man with a dream. It isn't his fault that the dream requires my cooperation."

"But you *are* angry."

"Well, my head says no, but my heart wants an apology."

She thought about that for a minute.

"I know a few parents like that myself," she said, finally.

I thought of my father out in Arizona, imagined him staring at me with hard, unforgiving eyes. I imagined myself staring back, trying to stare him down, but the longer I looked the more the image got confused with Irene Liston.

We went to a seafood restaurant on Wisconsin Avenue, a dark labyrinth of cozy little dining rooms decorated with tropical fish tanks. It was crowded with serious eaters. I had had a snack on the plane back from Rochester, but I was hungry again. I ordered a combination seafood platter—everything breaded and fried—and Jane ordered a cold crab salad.

"This may seem silly to you," Jane said, when the waitress had left us, "but I'm really excited."

"About what?"

"About being here with you. Having dinner in a restaurant with a presentable man. It's like a date. I haven't had a real honest-to-goodness date more than two or three times in my whole life."

"I find that hard to believe," I said.

"Then you still don't understand about figure skaters yet," she said. "Dating is one of many things we don't have much experience with."

"What are the others?"

"Oh, parties, football games. The senior prom. Just about everything a normal teenager would do for fun is outside the experience of a teenager who skates in competition. No time for it."

"Is that a universal experience?"

"Almost."

"You're not a teenager anymore," I pointed out.

"Doesn't matter. My schedule hasn't changed much. Up at five in the morning, work until ten or eleven at night. Six days a week, most weeks. Seven days a week, sometimes. When would I have a date?"

"On one of those rare nights off."

"All right, but with whom? When you're at the ice rink six nights of the week, when are you going to meet someone whom you might want to see socially?"

"How about one of your students?"

"Sixteen-year-old boys with acne? I don't think so. Besides, did you ever date your teacher? Yuck."

"I guess I see your point. And I think I'm flattered."

"Flattered?"

"You called me presentable. That's by no means a unanimous opinion."

She smiled. "Quite presentable," she said. "More than that, intelligent, witty, even charming in a way."

"Enough. I'm inflating like a balloon."

"All right."

She became serious so quickly that I was disappointed. Despite my protests, I would have enjoyed a bit more flattery. I had to take a long draw from my beer in order to hide my embarrassment.

After a moment, she said, "I have two questions."

"Okay. I'll try to have two answers."

"Question number one. Did the problem with your

windshield have something to do with Debbie? With this case?"

"Probably."

"What happened?"

"Somebody took some shots at me when I was driving over to the rink to see you."

"Whoa!" she said. "Are you serious?"

"Very."

"You mean someone tried to kill you? Over *Debbie?*"

"I know—it sounds absurd. But somebody definitely followed me along Beach Drive for about a mile, and I've got the windshield to prove it."

"Any idea who it was?"

I was surprised to discover that I did have an idea who it was, but I didn't want to commit myself yet.

"Ask me in a day or two," I said.

"All right. Ready for question number two?"

"Shoot," I said. "On second thought, I've had enough shooting for one night. Just ask the question."

"Who killed Jack Dumas?"

"I don't know," I said. "A burglar, maybe. But that doesn't explain what Jack was doing in a strange house. I don't think it was a burglar. More often than not, murderers and their victims know each other, but I don't know who was in Dumas's social circle."

"I don't think he had one," she said. "I think he would have liked to be in Irene's circle, but he was outclassed."

"No, he wasn't in Wellington Hollister's league," I said.

"It wasn't a burglar," she said firmly. "I think it has to do with Debbie."

"So do I," I said. "I just can't figure out the connection."

"Somebody doesn't want her to continue skating," Jane said. "Jack did. Maybe they thought Irene would be persuaded to retire Debbie if Jack were dead."

"I don't have the impression Irene would be persuaded by disaster falling on someone else," I said. "I think she'd be pretty much impervious to the misfortunes of other people."

Jane thought a moment. "You're probably right. But maybe they didn't know that."

"On the other hand, who tampered with Debbie's skates, if it wasn't Dumas?" I said.

"Surely you don't think Jack did that."

"If I had to pick a suspect for that, right now I'd pick Dumas," I said. "I don't know what his motive was, but he certainly had the opportunity."

"Lots of people had the opportunity," she said. "People are coming and gong behind that rental counter all day."

"But could you work on those skate blades with a metal file and not be noticed? I can't see it. It had to be someone who wouldn't look out of place working on skates. Dumas fills the bill."

"I see what you mean," she said.

"On the other hand," I said, "if Dumas was behind all this, who killed him and why? That's the trouble with this case: there are too many 'on the other hands.' I can't find any realistic motive, and in its absence I'm grasping at any half-baked theory that pops into my head."

The food arrived then, and Jane plowed into her salad as if she hadn't eaten all day—as, I guess, she hadn't. I found myself wondering if she wasn't skimping on meals to stretch her money farther. Maybe she was having difficulty making the payments on her Porsche.

"Figure skating must be an expensive pursuit," I said.

She nodded vigorously.

"It is if you're serious about it," she said. "And I don't just mean serious competitively. I have some private pupils who spend a hundred dollars a week on recreational skating. These are grown men and women I'm talking about."

"How can you spend that much money on a hobby? What can you spend it on?"

She ticked off with her fingers. "Private instruction, for one. I charge ten dollars for twenty minutes of instruction. If you take a couple of lessons from me, and another couple of lessons a week from one or two other instructors, you've already spent forty dollars a week."

"Why would someone take lessons from more than one instructor?"

"That's like asking why someone would read more than one book. Different instructors specialize in different things. I don't teach dance very much, but there are instructors who are very good at it."

"All right. What else?"

"Group instruction. Some of my pupils do both.

Third, rink admission. Two or three dollars a night, and they keep going up. Some of my pupils come to the rink every night. Fourth, patch time."

"Patch time?"

"That's where you rent a small piece of clean ice so you can practice doing your figures."

"Those are the figure eights and stuff?"

"Right. Then there's skate sharpening, new blades, new boots, new dresses for the women, transportation costs. It all adds up after a while."

"I'm beginning to get the idea," I said.

"Not everybody spends that much, but you'd be surprised how many do."

"Why do they do it?" I asked. "Do grown men and women still harbor dreams of Olympic gold medals?"

"Not that they'd admit to," she said. "But there are separate competitions for adults, and there's a certain thrill to being able to skate better than your peers, at any age. Why do grownups play softball? It's the same thing."

"I see."

She had polished off the salad. She leaned back in her chair and smiled at me. The light from a fish tank bathed her face in a soft lavender glow. She looked like a carnival kewpie doll, illuminated by the lights of the midway.

"It isn't just competition," she said. "A lot of people skate in order to keep fit, but there's even more to it than that. There's the thrill of gliding on the ice, faster than you could possibly run, but with less effort than it takes to walk. When I'm skating for pleasure I like to swing out in wide, sweeping circles on my outside edges. If you get a good edge, you can make a perfect circle without moving a muscle. I love to ride that edge and see that circle being traced behind me, hearing that gritty sound of my blade cutting perfectly in the ice. That may not make sense to you, if you haven't done it yourself, but a skater would know what I'm talking about."

"What do you do on your day off?" I asked. "Go skating?"

She smiled once more. "Sometimes."

The wind was whipping the snow into a fine, talcum-like grit as we came out of the restaurant. Jane volunteered to drive me home, and I accepted.

"I live in Virginia," she said. "Foggy Bottom is right on my way."

On the Rock Creek Parkway, the oaks and hickories and chestnuts loomed out of the night as the headlights of the Porsche picked them out. As we passed each tree I imagined I saw a man in a sheepskin jacket stepping out with a gun in his hand.

No one took a shot at us, and soon we were puttering along Twenty-third Street, and then we were at my door, saying good-bye.

"Would you like to come up for coffee?" I asked.

"Yes," she said. "But no, thank you. There's a principle involved."

"What principle is that?"

"My principle. The principle that I should never get too involved with a man until I've had time to think about it thoroughly. So not tonight, thank you."

"All right."

"I mean, I'm tempted. But I want to think about it."

"Okay."

"It's not that I don't like you, or anything like that."

"I know. You find me quite presentable, in fact."

"Oh, dear. I suppose I'll never live that down. It's just that . . ."

"I know. Principle."

"Yes, that's—"

I leaned over and kissed her through the open window. The kiss lasted a reasonable length of time, and I detected no signs that she wanted me to speed it up. So I didn't.

"What was that for?" she asked when we finally broke for air.

"Principle," I said.

"It was a very long kiss."

"I'm a highly principled man."

She considered that for a long moment. "I have a lot to think about," she said finally.

She eased the Porsche away from the curb and drove off slowly down the street. At the corner she turned to the right, and then she was gone.

Chapter Ten

I climbed the stairs to my apartment feeling remarkably lightheaded. The feeling disappeared abruptly at my front door.

There was a light on inside my apartment.

I hadn't left it on.

Someone was in there. I could see the thin yellow line of light where the door refused to quite touch the threshold.

A chill trickled up my spine and burrowed in at the base of my neck.

All during dinner and all the way home, I had been worrying. The guy who had shot at me on the parkway was still at large. By accompanying her to a restaurant, I had thoughtlessly exposed Jane Borman to the same danger I had faced.

Fortunately, nothing had happened. Now I knew why. My assailant hadn't needed to waylay me somewhere on the road. He knew where I lived. And he knew that, wherever I might go, sooner or later I would come home.

The hunt had not ended, after all. It had merely been suspended for a while.

There were no signs of tampering at the door, no signs of prying at the jamb. How had he gotten in?

What difference did it make?

I stood in the hallway outside my door and considered my options.

I was on the second floor of a three-story building. At the end of the hall was a window—narrow, but just big enough to squeeze through. I walked to the window as quietly as I could and looked down at the blacktop parking lot at the rear of the building. There was no big blue Pontiac, but he might have parked it on the street down the block. Or he might have stolen another car by now. I hadn't seen the Toyota with the foam rubber dice for several days, assuming it was the same man driving both cars.

To my right was another window—the window of my bedroom. The bedroom had once been a screened-in summer porch built as a sun room out over the rear portico of an old rowhouse. The porch had later been insulated and paneled in order to make it usable all year. The building had been converted to apartments.

My bedroom, therefore, jutted out at a forty-five-degree angle, about ten feet from where I stood. If I could get over to it, I could stand on the portico roof, remove the window screen, and enter the apartment through the bedroom. If I could do it quietly enough, it would give me the advantage of surprise.

Assuming, also, that I hadn't locked the window that morning before I left for the office. I couldn't remember for sure, but I didn't think I had. The odds were in my favor.

I knew already how I would get over there, across

the ten-foot gap. My landlady had strung a twenty-foot length of clothesline in the basement storage room just the week before.

Thanking providence that Mrs. Baxter was too cheap to buy a clothes dryer for tenants, I crept to the basement as quickly as I could go. The clothesline was hanging right where I had last seen it. I untied it and brought it back upstairs in a tight coil, taking care not to creak on the ancient wooden stairs.

At the window, I tied one end of the line to the radiator. It wasn't putting out much heat, but I shut it off anyway, to eliminate the possibility that the heat might burn through the cord. I tied the other end in a bowline around my waist—the things you learn in Boy Scouts stay with you all your life—and slipped out the window.

My sneakers gripped the wall fairly well, but they let the cold winter air pass through to my feet. The rough-textured old bricks provided plenty of traction, however, and inch by inch I worked my way across the outside wall to the portico roof, playing out the cord as I went.

My left foot finally appeared to be within reach of the roof. I held the line as taut as I could manage and worked my foot over until I could just feel the aluminum gutter that ran along the eaves. The gutter wouldn't hold my weight, of course. I'd have to get beyond that.

I worked a little farther until my foot met the unyielding surface of the roof itself. With a sigh, I eased myself over onto it.

It held my weight.

I eased off on the clothesline and turned my attention to the bedroom window, where I discovered a new problem.

Storm windows.

I had been complaining about the lack of storm windows for months. Now, barely three weeks before Christmas, they had finally been put up.

They hadn't been up when I had left the apartment that morning. They would be a minor problem, because I would have to remove them and lay them somewhere with care.

There was a narrow space where the roof joined the house, and it was small enough that storm windows might fit there nicely. I grasped the aluminum window frame firmly at the bottom and lifted it carefully off its hooks. I carried it gingerly to the corner of the roof and set it into the space. It fit with a little room on either side.

I returned to try the double-hung bedroom window. It resisted but finally rose grudgingly to the top. With the window open, I could hear the sound of my television set blaring from the living room. It was tuned to the eleven o'clock news. My visitor, whoever he was, had a lot of nerve. Maybe he wanted to know what the police had found out about the murder of Jack Dumas. Jack the Ripper probably kept a scrapbook.

I boosted myself up onto the windowsill and began worming my way through the opening.

I had nearly made it through the window when the clothesline snapped. It whipped between my legs and out the window, and I heard a thud as it snagged the storm window on the roof. I listened in dismay as the window slid down the roof and clattered over the side and crashed to the parking lot below.

The intruder suddenly shut off the television set in the living room. There was breathless silence everywhere.

I wriggled the rest of the way through the window and slid to the floor beside my bed. I lay there quietly, hoping that no one would come through the door.

Too late. I could hear him moving already, and he was moving in my direction.

If I could close the window, maybe he wouldn't realize that someone had come in. One look at the open window, and there could be no doubt.

I sprang to the window and pulled with all my might, but it resisted my efforts to close it.

Stupid window. The intruder was at the door. I gave the sash one last hard, desperate yank.

The bedroom light was switched on. It caught me spread-eagle before the opening.

I turned slowly to face the intruder and heard my sister say, "What in heaven's name do you think you're doing?"

"Praying," I said.

"What?"

"You asked what I'm doing. I'm praying. It's a new religion. You stand at the window and face the setting sun and break storm windows as a sacrifice to the spirit of winter. It's primitive, I know, but you've always known I was a primitive."

"Your window faces south, not west," she said. "And the sun's been down for hours. You've been sneaking into your own apartment. In heaven's name, why?"

"It's my apartment. If I want to come through the chimney, that's strictly up to me—and perhaps Mrs. Baxter. How did *you* get in here?"

"Mrs. Baxter let me in," she said. "I told her I was waiting for you to get home, and she said it was silly for me to wait outside in the hall when I could be waiting inside with a fire and a glass of wine."

That had the ring of truth to it. My landlady was my sister's biggest fan. She watched the news every night at six and eleven in order to catch a glimpse of her reporting from an embassy party or interviewing an old woman whose dog smoked a pipe. No story, no matter how trivial, was an unimportant story to Mrs. Baxter, as long as Susan was reporting it. She would point me out to her friends and introduce me as Susan's little brother. I always thought I was lucky that she hadn't given Susan her own key to my apartment, and I strongly suspected that she rented to me only because I was related to Susan.

"You must be cold," Susan said. "Come sit by the fire and have some wine."

She turned away and sauntered back to the living room. I followed sheepishly.

"I'm afraid you didn't have much of a wine selection to choose from," she said over her shoulder. "Your supply is low. I had to make do with a Napa Valley white zinfandel. You're out of your good wines."

The Napa Valley white zinfandel, I thought ruefully, *was* my good wine. It was the best wine I had ever owned. I had bought two bottles of it, and they had cost fourteen dollars apiece, which was roughly twice as much as I had ever paid for a wine before. The first bottle had been so good—extraordinarily good, so much better than my highest expectations—that I had decided to save the second bottle for a special occasion. I had envisioned that occasion involving a festive, celebratory atmosphere and a beautiful woman.

My sister was a beautiful woman, but she wasn't quite what I had had in mind.

She patted the place on the sofa beside her, and I sat meekly where she indicated. She poured me a glass of my liquid gold.

"This is actually quite a good wine," she said. "Considering that it's so inexpensive it's really quite pleasant. How did you come to buy it?"

"By the label," I said.

"Of course by the label, silly. I know that. But how did you know that Clourot was a name to look for? It's not a vineyard that I've ever heard about, and I like to think I know a little something about wine. I've certainly never considered you a connoisseur."

"I picked it because of the label," I explained again. "It was blue and yellow, and it had an interesting line drawing of a California-Spanish manor house. I thought it was an attractive label, so I bought it."

She looked at me in what I took to be horror.

"Are you telling me that you bought the wine because the label was *pretty?*"

"Well, distinctive. It caught my eye. I was rolling

my shopping cart down the aisle at Giant, and I saw the label nut of the corner of my eye. So I stopped."

"Distinctive?"

"Well, maybe assertive is a better word."

She stared at me for a second and then burst into laughter. "Marvelous," she said. "A clever answer." The wineglass shook in her hand as she laughed, and the wine splashed over the rim a bit. When Mrs. Baxter complained about the stain on the carpet, I could at least console her with the fact that it was an *expensive* wine stain. Maybe she'd forgive me if I told her Susan had caused it.

"What do you want, Susan?" I asked.

"What do you mean?"

"This isn't a social call," I said. "You don't call on me socially. And you didn't come to seek my advice on wine. And you didn't bring your latest boyfriend for my approval. So why did you come?"

She favored me with her sober, hard-eyed look. "My, aren't we cynical today," she said.

"Look," I said. "I'm not in your class. We don't run in the same social circles, and my work embarrasses you. I enjoy your company, whatever the reason, but I just can't figure what the reason might be."

"Hasn't it occurred to you that I might want to see you?" she asked. "After all, you're my brother."

"No."

"Why not?"

"You never visit me unless you want something."

"I find that assertion terribly offensive," she said. "I should leave you here to wallow in your loneliness."

I waited silently. After a moment she picked up the bottle and refilled her wineglass.

"Fortunately," she said, "I'm not as petty as all that. I can rise above your churlish nature."

"Oh, good," I said. And I was surprised to discover that I was secretly relieved.

"Actually, I *do* want something," she said.

"What do you want?"

"Your happiness."

She took a long sip from her wineglass and looked at me expectantly over the rim. It was my turn either to bite or to wait. I waited.

"I want you to come home with me," she said.

"I'm already home."

"I want you to come with me to Arizona for Christmas."

"Arizona isn't home," I said. "Not for me, not for you."

"Your mother and father are at home there," she said.

"Pop doesn't want to see me again," I said. "And Mom mostly wants what Pop wants."

"They're your family," she said. "Don't you feel anything for them, anymore?"

"Of course I do," I said. "But that doesn't matter. Pop and I can't stay in the same room for thirty minutes without going for each other's throats. What kind of Christmas would that be? I can't believe you'd want to subject Mom to that, or Pop, or yourself."

"It doesn't have to be that way," she said quietly.

"Maybe not. But that's the way it's always been."

"You could try harder," she said, even more softly.

The tone of her voice surprised me. I glanced up and saw a tear in the corner of one eye. The tear began sliding down over her cheekbone as I watched, gathering momentum on the downhill side. I watched in fascination. I couldn't remember the last time I had seen Susan cry.

"I know you're bitter," she said. "And your reasons are obviously justifiable, as far as you're concerned. I don't know; I was away in college when you and Dad had your disagreements. Then I was working and living on my own. I missed it all, so I don't know who was right and who was wrong. But I do know that this is killing Mom, and it's killing Dad, too. Even if he doesn't admit it. You could try harder to make up with him."

"So could he."

"You're killing him," she said again.

"That's not fair."

"You don't know!" she said. "You sit here in your little apartment in your splendid isolation and imagine what's happening. You don't know what's happening. You can't know. You're working out of your memory and imagination and anger. Where are your facts? What kind of investigator are you?"

"They can always come here," I said in protest. "I'll even put them up."

"But they won't. You know that."

"So why should I go to them? Why is it my responsibility if it isn't theirs?"

"Because you love them," she said. "For the same reason you put up with me even when I'm nagging you about your profession and your curious lack of ambition. Because they are your family, as I am, and certain obligations come with the territory."

"Duty before pleasure," I said.

"Duty *is* pleasure," she said. "That's one of the rules."

"How very Presbyterian of you."

She smiled ironically. "Contrary to what you may believe about me, Leo, I am not ashamed of being a puritan."

It was a curious form of puritanism she practiced, I thought, but I said nothing.

"Besides, how do you know Dad won't feel different about you now?"

"He's had several years to feel different about me. It doesn't seem to take."

"But things have changed. I'm sure he's thought about this."

"What things have changed? Has he quit watching baseball?"

She looked at me. "You don't know about the stroke?"

"Stroke?"

"Last month," she said. "He was playing golf, and suddenly he collapsed on the green while he was waiting his turn to putt. Didn't Mom write to you about it?"

"I haven't heard from her in months."

"Then Dad must have told her not to. She must have been counting on me to tell you."

"How is he? I gather he recovered."

"He's partially paralyzed, but the doctors think it might go away in time."

"So he's all right."

"He's doing as well as can be expected." She flashed me a grim smile. "But a thing like this makes you stop and take stock of your life. Petty disagreements start to look pretty small."

"Maybe."

She stood up, drained her wine, and set the glass gently on the coffee table.

"I have to go," she said. "I'm on the morning shift." She picked up the Cashmere coat she had draped over the back of the sofa. I wondered what John Knox or John Calvin would have said about her coat.

"Give it some thought, Leo," she said. "Don't rule it out too quickly. If you decide to come with me, I'll even pay your airfare to Phoenix."

"*If* I decide to go, I'll pay my own way."

She studied me carefully, at close range. "Then you'll consider it?" she asked.

"I'll consider it."

She kissed me on the cheek, like a maiden aunt, and walked to the door. When she reached it, she handed me the extra key to the apartment.

"Please return this to Mrs. Baxter for me," she said.

"I will."

"By the way," she said. "Since you were sneaking into your own apartment through the window, I assume you had a good reason. Are you in some sort of danger?"

"It would appear so."

"Is it related to your investigation business?"

"I think so."

I thought she would say something brittle and witty.

Instead, she merely shook her head, smiled gently, and left the apartment. She closed the door quietly. It wasn't until I had turned the deadbolt lock behind her that I finally heard her footsteps clicking away down the hall.

Chapter Eleven

Arthur Seagram turned out to be a shriveled little man who was probably about fifty but seemed older. I found him in Dumas's office the following morning, working on the books. He was a funny sight—a tiny man with big red hands that looked like miniature hams, gripping a stub pencil in his fist like a first-grader.

He tore himself away with some reluctance after I explained who I was and what I was doing.

"What do you want to know?" he said irritably. "I'm up to here in problems this morning."

"I'd like to know something about Jack Dumas."

"What sort of thing? I hired him to run this business for me. We weren't buddies."

"How long had he worked for you? Where did he come from? Did he have recommendations? That's the sort of thing I'm looking for."

He sighed. Loudly. "I told all that to the police," he said. "Several times, in fact, to several different policemen."

"I'd appreciate it if you'd tell me, too."

He studied me the way a cat studies a small rodent.

"You said Irene Liston hired you to protect her daughter. What's your interest in Dumas?"

"Dumas was interested in Irene, and I'm trying to figure out why."

The brown eyes narrowed. "You're sure of that?"

"He was conducting some sort of investigation into her past shortly before he died."

"You mean blackmail."

"Maybe."

The wizened face sagged, and he propped it up with hamhock hands. "That's great," he said. "That's all I need."

"What do you mean?"

He laid his yellow pencil on the ledger book to mark his place and closed the book on it gently.

"That's all I need," he said, again. "A little blackmail would just make my day. I wonder how many other of my customers he was working on."

"I don't know yet that blackmail was his intent," I said.

"It stands to reason, doesn't it? Besides, it's consistent with everything I've found out in the last day or so. There's no question the man was stealing me blind. I'm not surprised to find he was also extorting a little something extra from the clientele."

"How was he stealing from you?"

"He was skimming," he said. "Taking a little off the top here, a little more there, and putting it in his pocket."

"Are you sure?"

"Sure enough. I started looking over the books yesterday, when I learned he was dead. He was cagy about it, but I'm coming up short. I haven't finished checking things out, you understand, but I don't think I'm going to find the missing money."

"How much is missing?"

"So far," he said, "I make it at about twenty thousand dollars."

"That's a lot of money."

He nodded glumly. "It won't break me, but it may mean the difference between a profit and a loss this year. It's come closer than that before."

"How did he do it?"

"Like I said, he was cagy. An order of skate boots would come in from the manufacturer, and there'd be one or two pairs less than he paid for. Or he would overpay on fuel for the Zamboni—I don't have a long-term contract, and it's hard to keep up with the price changes if you're not watching every day. He was nickel-and-diming me on concessions. There wasn't much falling between the cracks at any one time, but it added up."

"Why didn't you catch him at it?"

"I wasn't watching."

"This is your business."

"This is *one* of my businesses," he said. "Mostly, I'm in the construction business. Of course, that's gone in the toilet the last few years, but it's what I know best. I wound up owning a skating rink by accident. I built it for a guy, and he defaulted, and it fell into my hands. I can't sell it, business being the way it is, so I'm stuck with it. I don't know a lot about skating rinks, but I know enough to recognize a high-cost, low-margin operation when I see one. Some of these costs, though, are just a little *too* high."

"Would you mind telling me when Dumas came to work for you? Was he recommended?"

"I certainly didn't go out on the street and rustle people, if that's what you mean. He came with references. Good ones, too, from the looks of them."

"Did you check them out?"

"I checked a couple of them, but I did it mostly just to make sure he had worked where he said he had. I didn't go in for a lot of intensive investigation."

"I gather nobody volunteered any derogatory information, though."

"If he did to others what he did to me, they didn't see fit to tell me about it," he said. "Probably nobody else gave him as much opportunity as I did."

"When did he go to work for you?"

"About a year ago," he said. "My previous manager had a heart attack a year ago last June and dropped dead in his driveway. I advertised for a replacement, and pretty soon Dumas turned up on my doorstep with a résumé and references."

"Where did he come from?"

"Cleveland. He had a flowery letter from a rink up in Shaker Heights."

"Do you still have his résumé?"

"I think so." He opened the top drawer of the filing cabinet behind him and pawed through it for a moment.

"It isn't here," he said. "He must have pulled it to keep me from checking up on him again."

"Thanks, anyway," I said.

"Mind if I ask you a question?" Seagram said.

"Go ahead."

"Dumas wrote you a retainer check. How much was it?"

"A thousand dollars."

He shook his head and went back to his work. "He wrote twelve hundred on the check stub," he said.

On the ice, Jane was watching a Vietnamese woman, in horn-rimmed glasses, execute a series of turns. I knocked on the glass and waved to Jane, and she smiled and wiggled her fingers at me. She spoke to her pupil briefly and skated over to where I stood.

"How are you?" she asked, slightly breathless.

"Fine. And you?"

"Oh, I feel very good," she said. "Supergood. Thank you for dinner last night."

"My pleasure. Let's do it again. How about to-night?"

"I can't tonight. Ballet class."

"You take ballet?"

"Modern dance, too. I like to think it helps my skating, but mostly I do it because it's fun. How's your investigation coming?"

"I'm beginning to get some ideas," I said. "Do you still have the videotape of Debbie's fall?"

"It's at home. Want to see it?"

"Very much. Could you bring it in tomorrow?"

"All right. If it's important, I'll go home today and get it. I'll cancel a class."

"Tomorrow's soon enough," I said.

* * *

My car had been towed away from the parking lot finally, and taken to a garage nearby where they were familiar with it. There were still shards of glass scattered over the icy pavement. They could have replaced the glass on the spot, but I wanted them to do something about the bullet holes in the trunk, too. It's bad business to drive around town in a car that's obviously been shot at.

I caught a cab back to the office. Georgie was at her desk when I arrived. I marvelled continually at my good fortune in finding her. I had hired her originally as a secretary-receptionist, but she had become a good deal more than that: administrative aide, accountant, confidante, and strategist. If she had a fault it was that she was too beautiful—so beautiful I sometimes found it distracting.

If I ever let on, of course, I would lose all those remarkable qualities for which I had hired her. I didn't think her husband would like it much, either.

"Where have you been this morning?" she asked. "You usually call and let me know when you're going to be late."

"Sorry. I've been at the skating rink."

"Lt. Barlow wants you to call him," she said. "And the garage called to say your car would be ready around noon. They asked if you'd been in an accident of some sort."

"It was no accident," I said. I went to my office and called Barlow. He was out of his office again, but I got Geisele instead.

"The lieutenant's gonna be sorry he missed you, McFarlin," Geisele said. "He really looks forward to your calls. I thought he was gonna cry when he came in this morning and found that you tried to call him last night."

"I'm a sparkling conversationalist."

"A born storyteller," he said. "I really like that story about how you went to the front door of that house the other day and didn't go in. Barlow liked it, too."

"Good," I said. "I got another story for him today." I told him what had happened to me on the Rock Creek Parkway the night before.

"What makes you worth shooting?" Geisele said.

"Darned if I know," I said. *And maybe darned if I don't,* I thought.

I hung up and leaned back in my chair. Outside my window I could see Christmas shoppers and office workers bustling back and forth as if the future of the free world depended on their successful acquisition of a jade bracelet from Hecht's, or two pounds of French-roast coffee beans from M. E. Swing Co., or tickets to "A Christmas Carol" at Ford's Theater. It was still an hour before noon, but the sidewalks were already crowded with people.

Sooner or later I would have to do Christmas shopping of my own. I wondered idly what I could get for my father, aside from a necktie or a major league baseball contract.

Barlow called back about twenty minutes later.

"Sergeant Geisele told me your story," he said. "You must really learn to be more careful when you're driving through the park."

"I'll keep that in mind."

"Did you see your assailant's face?"

"At a distance. I didn't take notes, though."

"I imagine you didn't. Would you recognize the man again? I assume it was a man."

"I don't know."

"Which question is that an answer to?"

"Both, I think."

"Very well," he said. "Why don't you come down this afternoon and look at some mug books. Perhaps you'll have some luck."

"Promise not to lock me up?"

"I won't lock you up unless it seems advisable for your own protection," he said. "But right now I'm of two minds about that."

I didn't get lucky. I spent a couple of hours looking at mug shots but saw no one who even vaguely resembled the man who had shot at me in Rock Creek Park. When I finally called it quits, I had a backache and a headache from the chair and the lighting in the police station, but I didn't have any information that I hadn't come in with.

Handyman Barlow accompanied me to the sidewalk.

"I suppose you're certain that this incident actually occurred?" he said. "You had a hard day yesterday. Perhaps you fell asleep and dreamed the whole thing."

"I'll give you the name of my garage," I said, "and you can ask the condition of my windshield and rear window when they picked the car up this morning. You can also ask them about the bullet hole in my trunk."

"I don't think I'll bother," he said. "I don't really care, you know. I was just making idle conversation."

I left him at the corner and walked to the nearest subway station, where I caught the train in the direction of Capitol Hill. It was a red line train, which dropped me at Union Station, and I had to walk quite a distance. I went to the Library of Congress and spent about an hour looking at the rule books of the United States Figure Skating Association and at back issues of *Skating* magazine. In a 1974 issue I found a couple of fleeting references to an up-and-coming young pairs team named Kreeger and Liston. I came away with confirmation that the team of Kreeger and Liston had actually existed, but nothing else.

At three o'clock I called my office.

"Thank goodness," Georgie said. "Irene Liston just called. She's trying to reach you."

"I'm on Capitol Hill right now," I said. "I'll drop by her office."

"No, she's at home, and she sounds upset."

"What's the problem?"

"Somebody got into her house and left a grisly little present for Debbie in the living room. A dead rat in a shoe box."

"In the living room?"

"Right in the middle of the rug," she said.

Way to go, McFarlin. Spend an hour reading old magazines in the library while somebody's playing dirty tricks on your client.

"Call her back," I said. "Tell her I'm on my way."

* * *

The cab took me through Georgetown and out the other side. The driver deposited me on a quiet, tree-lined street in a neighborhood known as Glover Park. Although most of the District's safer neighborhoods are being priced out of the reach of the middle class, Glover Park had managed to hold on against the odds.

Irene Liston lived in a small pseudo-Tudor house, which was set back from the street on a narrow lot. The sidewalk in front was cracked and pitted from years of frost heaves. An ancient hickory tree stood patiently on the front lawn, awaiting the windstorm or lightning bolt that would bring it down.

Irene Liston was waiting for me at the door, looking pale and shaken but with a glint in her eye.

"Where have you been?" she asked, heatedly.

"Doing research."

"Get in here quickly," she said. "And look at this."

We passed through a close little foyer with a glossy hardwood floor into a living room that wasn't much bigger than the foyer. The shoe box sat in the middle of the floor. The name of an expensive brand of women's shoes was emblazoned on the end of it in particularly florid script.

I knelt and looked inside. The lid was off. The rat lay on its side, cushioned in the sort of tissue paper shoes come wrapped in. It wasn't a very big rat, probably not yet adult. Someone had tied a wide red ribbon around its neck, complete with a bow. Blood had trickled from the corner of the animal's mouth. Poisoned, probably.

"I found it about an hour ago," she said. "I left it right where it was and called you immediately."

"The lid was on it when you found it?"

"Yes. I thought it was a pair of my own shoes until I picked it up. I buy this brand a lot."

"Was there a note?"

"A note?"

"Yes. You know, a little slip of paper with 'Death to Debbie Liston' or something of the sort written on it?"

"There was no note. I do not like your tone, Mr. McFarlin."

"I know. I don't like it much myself, right now, Mrs. Liston. I'm mad at myself. Where's Debbie?"

"In her room. I didn't want her to see this, but she did."

"Is she taking it all right?"

"Well enough."

I started for the stairs. Irene followed and laid a restraining hand on my arm.

"You can't go up there. I'll call her down. We can all sit in the living room. I'll move the rat to the kitchen."

I shook my head. "I want to talk to her alone."

"She's my daughter," she said. "We have no secrets from each other."

"That's wishful thinking," I said. "Everybody has secrets. That's why we have private investigators."

Her room was easy to find. There was a poster of Tara Lipinski on the door, a magazine gatefold with a crease at her midriff and a hole where the staple had been. I had seen a similar poster in Dumas's house. I hadn't given much thought to the muscular development of figure skaters, but I thought the poster girl looked compact and powerful, and strangely fragile, as well.

I knocked. No answer. Knocked again.

"Debbie, it's Leo McFarlin. Could we talk a minute?"

No answer. I took a deep breath and opened the door.

She lay on her stomach on a yellow-flowered bedspread, with her face buried in the pillow. The dominant color in the room was yellow, from the telephone on the bedside table to the frilly curtains on the window. She had pulled down the shade on the windowsill, and the late-afternoon sunlight filtered through and deepened the yellow aura. Some decorator had probably planned it that way.

"Would you mind sitting up? I'd like to see your face when I talk to you." I sounded like my mother.

She rolled over slowly, and I could see the redness around her eyes where the tears had been. It seemed to make her blue eyes even bluer.

"Is there something you'd like to tell me?" I asked.

The blue eyes stared at me. Her mouth formed words. She whispered so softly that I couldn't catch what she said.

"I'm sorry, Debbie. I didn't hear what you said."

"You know," she said, louder this time.

"What do I know, Debbie?"

"You know," she said again.

"What?" I said. "What do I know? Tell me about it."

She opened her mouth to speak, but did not. She turned away from me.

"Nothing," she said. "Go away."

I stood up, feeling a mixture of loss and gratitude. The telephone beside the bed rang and then stopped abruptly as it was picked up downstairs.

"If you want to talk to me, you know how to reach me," I said uselessly. I put my card on the table next to the phone and stepped out of the room.

Downstairs, Irene was listening on the phone. When she saw me, she waved frantically and pointed at the earpiece. I turned and hurried back to Debbie's room.

Debbie lifted her head in surprise as I re-entered the room, but I put my finger to my lips to silence her and lifted the receiver.

". . . . message wasn't lost on you," the voice on the other end of the line was saying. "We got in once, and we can get in and do it again."

"But why?" I heard Irene ask.

"It doesn't matter why," the voice said. "As long as you get the message, that's all that counts."

He had taken some pains to disguise his voice with a handkerchief, but I recognized Philip Lanham, and I had no doubts that Irene recognized it, too. I was disappointed in ways I had not expected.

The line clicked and went dead.

Irene was waiting for me when I came back downstairs.

"It was Philip," she said triumphantly.

"I know."

"I'll call the police and have him arrested."

"Let me talk to him first," I said, slipping on my jacket. "Something about this still doesn't feel right. I can't believe he would be involved in anything that would hurt Debbie."

"Isn't it obvious by now?"

"Maybe not. In any case, I want to know who's in this with him. He said '*we* mean business.' "

A cab took me to the garage near my apartment where my car was waiting. I picked it up and drove toward Virginia, where Philip Lanham's ice rink was located. I would have to begin looking for him there.

I passed under the terrace of the Kennedy Center. From there I could look out at the Potomac River, choked with ice. It was early in the winter for ice, normally. Maybe the ice age was returning. We'd certainly had an inordinate amount of snow so far.

Out on the river, a seagull wheeled and dove over an isolated patch of open water. The gull landed briefly on the surface of the ice, then took off again. I could sense his frustration as I sped by in my car. I was feeling it myself.

As I crossed Memorial Bridge into Virginia, the dark mass of Arlington Cemetery loomed ahead of me in the dusk, and I could see the flame flickering at the Kennedy grave.

An unhappy thought occurred to me. There had been a lot of guilt in the look that Debbie had given me. A lot of guilt. I tried out the idea of Debbie Liston as the murderer of Jack Dumas. I found, not unexpectedly, that I didn't much care for it.

Chapter Twelve

It took a little while, but I finally managed to talk the rink manager in Springfield into giving me Philip's address.

It was upstairs in an old Cape Cod–style house in Alexandria, in a neighborhood of older houses that had been converted into apartments. There were four apartments in the building—two on the main floor and two above—and the listing on the mailbox inside the front door indicated that Philip had one of the upstairs units. The big apartment on the ground floor, I assumed, belonged to his coach.

He came to the door only moments after my knock. When he recognized me, he tried to slam the door shut again. I hit the door hard with the flat of my hand and drove it back in his face. He staggered backward into the room, and I was inside with him before he could stop me.

"What are you doing?" There was fear in his eyes.

"I came for a visit. We have a lot to talk about."

"Get out!"

"In due course," I said. I grabbed his shirtfront and pulled him up short, gangster-movie style, as I kicked the door shut behind me. It made a satisfying bang as it slammed.

He decided to resist. He pulled away from me, and I let go of his shirt. He sprawled on his back on a faded sofa against the far wall. I followed him and rested my knee on his gut.

"You and me, Philip, we need to talk," I said. Tough guy, McFarlin. So tough he puts the subjects of his sentences into the objective case. That oughta scare the suspect.

Philip wasn't up to criticizing my grammar. "Talk about what?"

"Let's start with your phone conversation with Irene Liston," I said.

"I don't know what you're talking about."

"Let me see if I can help you remember," I said. "You had a handkerchief over your mouth, and you said, 'Let this be a warning to you.' Remember now?"

He reached up to claw my face, but I grabbed his arm and twisted him around onto his stomach, with his arm behind his back. I planted my knee in the small of his back and twisted his arm hard.

"I could break your arm pretty easily," I said. "I've got about twenty pounds on you, and I've probably beat people up more recently than you have. I'm not as rusty."

He squealed and squirmed, and I increased the pressure of my knee on his back.

"Maybe breaking your arm is a bad idea," I said. "Maybe I should break your ankle instead. How'd you like to sit out the winter skating season in front of the television set, with your foot in a cast?"

I could feel the fight going out of him. He sagged beneath me on the couch.

"Good boy," I said. "You can't beat me without an advantage, and I don't intend to give you one. You might as well relax."

His head slumped down to the sofa like a marionette with the strings cut.

"Want to tell me about it?"

"All right," he said. "But let me sit up. I can't talk in this position."

I eased my pressure on his back, and he squirmed around, reaching for my face with his free hand. I bore down on him again, and he gave up the effort.

"Naughty, naughty," I said, and pressed him deeper into the sofa. "Are you quite through now?"

He nodded silently. I stood up and moved away from him as he, in turn, moved to the far end of the sofa and looked away from me.

"Why did you call Irene Liston this afternoon?" I asked.

"I wanted to borrow a cup of flour," he said. He glared at me defiantly.

"I should have broken your ankle, after all."

"You don't frighten me," he said. "Big tough man. You don't scare me at all."

I moved toward him. He began backing away, but the attitude of defiance remained.

"Go ahead," he said. "Break my leg. I'll hit you with a lawsuit so fast it'll make your head swim."

I hesitated, considering the possibilities. This wasn't the way it was supposed to work. Did I *really* want to break his ankle? No, I probably didn't. Or rather, I

did, but it would be the surest way to defeat my ultimate purpose, which was to get information. I might
obtain the information I came for, but it probably
wouldn't be worth the trouble. And he was right: I
was on pretty shaky legal ground. I could wind up in
jail for assault and battery. I would lose my license.
Even if I obtained the information I wanted, I would
be unable to make use of it.

And there was another issue involved. Did I really
want to think of myself as someone who went around
breaking the arms and legs of amateur figure skaters?
What kind of reputation was that?

"The heck with it," I said, and turned away from
him.

"Get out." he said smugly. "Get out of here before
I call the police!"

His eyes held the same glitter of malice and con-
tempt I had seen in Irene Liston when she had recognized Philip's voice on the telephone. There was a
lot of hate between them, and I was caught in the
middle.

"I'm surprised at you, Philip," I said. "I expected
better of you than this."

But he was eager to press his advantage. "I warned
you," he said. He strode to the telephone and opened
the telephone directory. He ran his finger down the
page to find the number and dialed it. He could have
called 911, I thought, but I didn't think it was my
place to suggest it.

"Police?" he said. "I want to file a complaint. I'm
being harassed."

They put him on hold. When they did, I said: "Of

course, you realize that I'll tell them *why* I'm harassing you. I'll tell them I recognized your voice on the telephone. And I have a witness."

He turned away from me. I continued talking to the back of his head. "Harassment is a serious offense, but so is extortion. And when you do it over the telephone, it's a federal offense."

There was a chair by the telephone, and he sank into it, the receiver still in his hand. I could hear a male voice speaking to him through the receiver. After a moment he raised the phone to his mouth and spoke back to the voice at the other end.

"Never mind," he said, and hung up.

"What do you want?" he asked.

"I want to know who's in this with you, and why."

"Nobody," he said. "It's just me. I was angry with Irene—I have ample reason to be angry with Irene— and I wanted to get back at her."

I shook my head. "It doesn't wash. Somebody tampered with Debbie's skates, and it wasn't you. You couldn't get within five hundred feet of the ice rink without somebody spotting you. Irene would have nailed your hide to the wall if you had shown your face around there."

"All right," he said. "Jack Dumas did that. It was the two of us."

"I don't buy that, either," I said. "And even if it's true, who killed Dumas? You? And why?"

"Not me."

"Then who? Why?"

"I don't know. Maybe they thought he was a burglar. He wasn't killed at home, was he? I read in the paper that he was killed somewhere in the District, but Jack lived in Maryland."

"What was he doing in that house?"

"I don't know," he said. "Just go away and leave me alone."

"Maybe I should tell Debbie about this," I said. "Maybe she'll have some ideas about what's going on."

He waved his hand at me limply. "Tell her anything you darn well please," he said. "Just go away."

"All right, Philip," I said. "I'll go now. But stay close to home. I may want to talk to you again."

" 'Bye-bye," he said.

I didn't go straight home. I stopped off in a bar not far from my apartment and drank a beer. That helped a little.

Afterward, I felt the need for a restroom.

The men's rooms in Washington used to be covered with graffiti, much of it surprisingly political. But those were the old days, a couple of years ago, when Washington was a place where people lived. Now it's a place where technicians live: a habitat for those creatures who spend their lives writing reports and running numbers through computers.

There was only one message scrawled on the wall of this restroom, and it was so small that I almost missed it. It was written lightly in pencil, and it said: "COBOL LOVES FORTRAN."

I left the bar feeling slightly depressed.

* * *

"It has occurred to me, Leo," Handyman Barlow said, "that you are not entirely suited to this profession of yours. You could have asked me all these questions earlier this afternoon, when you were in my office."

"They didn't occur to me when I was in your office."

"That," said Barlow, "is my point."

We were sitting in a cocktail lounge in a Dupont Circle hotel, one of those increasingly rare places that employed a jazz pianist. I had put on a jacket and tie for the occasion. I had suggested that we meet for a drink, and Barlow had suggested the location. It was out of my price range, but Barlow had said he would pay. I was seeing how grownups lived, and they lived every bit as well as I had imagined.

"The trouble with you children," Barlow said, "is that you lack a sense of history."

"I got A's in history, all through school."

"Ah, but did you ever study Edward Kennedy Ellington?"

"I don't think so. Was he related to the president?"

"Perhaps, in a roundabout way, but I doubt that either would have acknowledged it. No, Leo, Edward Kennedy was the given name of the man the world now knows as Duke Ellington."

"What does he have to do with anything?"

"The pianist happens to be playing one of his compositions at the moment. It's called 'In a Mellotone.' Previously he played 'Take the A Train,' and 'Lush Life,' and 'Do Nothin' Till You Hear From Me.' Did any of these melodies impinge on your consciousness?"

"I knew I'd heard them before, if that's what you're getting at. I didn't know who wrote them, though."

"I won't go so far as to say that the gap in your knowledge about Ellington is due to the fact that he was a black man. I dare say you have a similar gap when it comes to Gershwin, or Arlen, or Hoagy Carmichael."

"I've heard of Gershwin—George, wasn't it—and Hoagy Carmichael. I've never heard of Arlen."

"I dare say. But you'll have heard his music. He wrote the music to *The Wizard of Oz*."

"I liked that movie. It wasn't cool for boys to like it, but I did. Especially 'Over the Rainbow.' "

"Arlen also wrote a song called 'The Man That Got Away,' " Barlow said. "Considering your recent exploits, I'd think you might take that as your personal theme song."

"I'm inexperienced with murder," I said. "I'll admit to that. I'll get the hang of it."

"If you live long enough."

"Oh, come on, Lieutenant. Haven't you ever forgotten a question you wanted to ask?"

"One question, yes," Barlow said. "But not two, and certainly not a dozen." He sipped his drink.

"You're lying."

"Yes, I am. Nevertheless, you've been remarkably clumsy. What is it that you want to know?"

"What have you found out about the man who was killed on Euclid Place?"

"Well, we know his name, of course, and his place of employment. He was killed by a single gunshot wound to the head, at extremely close range. He had been dead several hours. Other than that, I'm afraid, we don't know much. He hadn't been in the area very long, apparently. I should not be surprised to learn that he had a criminal record."

"Arthur Seagram thinks Dumas was skimming a little," I said.

"Who? Oh, yes, the little man who owns the rink. He told us that, too. That's one of the points that started me wondering."

"About what?"

"About money," Barlow said. "I've read in a number of places that figure skating is an extraordinarily expensive endeavor if one competes as an amateur in the top ranks. Anything that is expensive is usually attractive to a professional fundraiser with a little larceny in his blood."

"I don't follow you."

"Well, look at the way some charities operate. They bring in a professional fundraiser, who offers to help them get money for their cause in return for a percentage of the gross. He organizes a fund campaign, and because he organizes it he's in a position to control expenses and take a little out of the action there. Pretty soon, the fundraiser is making big money, but very little trickles down to the beneficiary. It wouldn't be hard to apply the same principles in this instance. You raise funds to send a skater to the national championships, for example, but you also raise a lot of money for your own use at the same time."

"I never would have thought of that sort of scam in this context," I said.

"But I did," he said. "And if I can think it, someone else is probably doing it."

"Jack Dumas?"

"Perhaps. Anytime you have people who need money, there's usually someone willing to supply it, for a price. And the more money you need, the higher will be the price."

"So who killed him?"

"We don't know that yet," he said.

"And why was he killed?"

"We don't know that, either."

"And you think *I'm* in the wrong business," I said.

"I *know* I'm in the wrong business," Barlow said. "Being a police officer in the District of Columbia is not the right business for anyone."

He knocked off the rest of his drink. I knocked off the rest of my drink. We both sat silently.

"Nice music," I said finally.

"It is not 'nice' music, Leo. Girl Scouts are nice. This is extraordinary music, or important music, or beautiful music, but not nice."

"Whatever."

"Is that all you wanted to see me about? To ask if we knew anything more about your murder victim?"

"Well, there is one thing more," I said.

"And what is that?"

"I want you to take me back to the scene of the crime," I said.

Chapter Thirteen

T he front door opened much more quietly than I had thought it would. A pale beam of light from a streetlamp snaked through the doorway and reflected off the newel post on the bannister directly in front of us.

The lights were off inside the house.

"Have a flashlight I could borrow?" I asked Barlow. He sighed, a heavy, exasperated sort of sigh, and flipped the wall switch by his hand. The hallway blazed with light.

"Oh," I said.

I crossed to the parlor door and flipped the wall switch there.

"I guess I thought the electricity would have been switched off by now," I said.

"It will be, tomorrow. Policemen find it easier to conduct their investigations if the electricity is working."

I looked instinctively to where I had seen the corpse of Jack Dumas sitting on my previous visit. He wasn't there, of course, and neither was the wing chair. Both had gone to the police lab.

"What are you looking for?" Barlow asked.

"A picture."

"Photograph?"

"Yes. Two skaters performing a death spiral. That's a figure skating maneuver."

"I know what a death spiral is. I have a six-year-old daughter."

"Great. Help me look for the picture, then. It's a black-and-white photo in a black plastic frame."

Barlow found it hanging in the bedroom, next to an ornate gilt-framed mirror. I removed it from the wall and sat on the edge of the bed to inspect it at close range.

"You think this is important," Barlow said, looking over my shoulder.

"I think so."

"Why?"

"That I don't know. But it was hanging in Dumas's office the first time I visited there. The next time I came, it was missing from the wall, and Dumas was missing, as well. I think somebody didn't want it to be recognized, and I'm assuming it was Dumas himself."

"Who else knew it was there?"

"Anybody who came to Dumas's office, I suppose. That could be a lot of people."

"So it must not have had any meaning to them. Why would it suddenly become important?"

"Oh, you know. You see something on the wall day after day without really thinking about it. Then somebody points it out to you, and you start to look at it in a whole new way. I happened to mention it to a guy who works at the rink, a guy named Martin.

Maybe he said something to Dumas, and Dumas suddenly realized he needed to dispose of the picture."

"So why didn't he just throw it away?"

"I don't know. Maybe it was important to him. Sentimental value, or something."

Barlow straightened up and headed for the bedroom door. "That's a lot of maybes," he said, shaking his head.

I couldn't blame him for being skeptical. I sat there, looking carefully at the photograph, asking it for answers. No answers came.

What did I know about the picture? Well, the girl, of course, was Irene Liston, nee Kreeger, at an earlier age. So the boy had to be Harry Liston, pairs skater and boy holdup man, late of Rochester, New York. It was presumably a publicity photo, though not a top-quality job—the sort of thing that an amateur organization with a limited publicity budget might commission from a local photographer. It was grainy and soft-edged, like a photo taken from the sidelines with a high-speed film and available light, rather than a crisp and glossy commercial publicity shot. It had survived all these years because it had been taken at just the right moment. It captured perfectly the tension and grace of a precisely executed death spiral.

How did it get to Washington, D.C.? Maybe Dumas had brought it with him. Maybe he had worked in Rochester, years earlier. Maybe Dumas had a thing for Irene. She would have been a teenager then, but Dumas would have been a lot younger, too.

Maybe somebody didn't want me to recognize Irene's face. But what difference would it make if I did?

Perhaps it was Harry's face that I wasn't supposed to recognize because I wasn't supposed to realize that Harry was still alive.

But I had figured that out already, and it didn't help. The photograph was a picture of a sixteen-year-old boy. By now, he would be in his thirties, and he could look quite different. If I had met him, I hadn't recognized him. And even if I had recognized him, it wouldn't explain why he would attempt to murder his own daughter.

Maybe the picture had been removed not to get it out of my sight, but someone else's. But whose?

I stood, tucking the picture under my arm, and descended the stairs. Barlow was waiting at the foot of the stairs. He pointed to the picture.

"That's evidence," he said.

"Of what?"

He shrugged; he didn't know, either. "If we have need of it, I'll want it back."

"Sure."

"You're barking up the wrong tree, anyway."

"Probably," I said, but I didn't think so.

"I've been thinking," he said. "If Dumas saved that picture because it was important to him, wouldn't he have kept it in his own house?"

"I'd have thought so. But Dumas obviously came here for some reason. So this house must have meant something to him, too."

"Maybe he rented it from the owner. We haven't been able to trace the owner, and the neighbors are not very helpful. Apparently, they didn't see much of him."

"Was the owner living here?"

"Nobody seems to know. You finished here?"

"I guess so," I said. "Let's get out of here. This place is depressing."

"Murder scenes tend to do that to you," he said.

The next morning was Saturday, the day Irene Liston expected her daughter to perform her skating routine in front of a crowd of people—one of whom might be planning to kill her. I was supposed to know the name of the bad guy by now.

Maybe my sister was right. Maybe I was in the wrong business again, for the third time in my life. Maybe that was to be my career: going through life picking out inappropriate careers, one at a time. They say everybody has a talent; maybe this was mine.

I called Peter Blenheim in Rochester. He answered on the first ring, even though it was Saturday, and he even sounded cheerful. Good for him.

"I've been hoping you would call," he said.

"Got something for me?"

"A little bit," he said. I could hear him rustling papers. "Harry Liston robbed a liquor store in Brighton, which is a suburb south of here. Liston wore a handkerchief over his face, like Jesse James, but somebody took down the license tag number on the getaway car, so they had a pretty good idea who did it."

"I gather it wasn't a stolen car."

Blenheim laughed. "It was his mother's car, if you can believe it. He was a real amateur. His mother claimed that the car had been stolen, but that explanation didn't hold up. The eyewitness who got the license plate—he was standing just outside the store in a phone booth—thought he saw a driver waiting behind the wheel, but he couldn't be sure. He didn't remember whether the robber got in behind the wheel or not."

"So they arrested Harry."

"Arrested him, booked him, and let him out on bail two days later. And a week after that, he drove into a bridge abutment on the New York State Thruway late at night."

"Didn't you tell me that he killed somebody in the robbery?"

"Yeah. He killed the owner, a Vietnamese man who had just bought the store not two weeks before. There was quite a bit of embarrassment when it came out that he'd been released on his own recognizance, but the criminal justice system seems to have survived the bad press."

A glimmer of an idea was taking shape in my mind. I tried to call it forward to look at it, without success.

"Was he driving his mother's car when he died?" I asked.

"No, he was driving his own car. His mother's car had been impounded by the cops. As evidence because of the license number."

Philip Lanham had said "we" on the telephone. *"Let this be a lesson to you. We mean business."*

I didn't think that was idle chatter. Whatever Philip was involved in, he had an accomplice. That accomplice had to be Harry Liston.

"How did Liston die?" I asked Blenheim.

"In the car crash, like I said."

"How did it happen?"

"It was late at night, he was driving fast on the thruway and went into a skid. The car turned over and slid on its roof for about fifty yards and then collided with a bridge abutment. Liston must have been doing about ninety when he flipped."

"Did the car burn?"

"Completely. And the corpse was a mess."

"Did they have any trouble with identification?"

"As a matter of fact, yes. There wasn't a whole lot of corpse to identify, and apparently Harry had never been to a dentist because there were no dental records to use. Fortunately, Harry's father was in town, and he made the identification."

Harry's father was mistaken, I thought. The police would figure a father knew his own son, but it might have been several years since they had seen each other. If the body was badly disfigured, Harry's father might not recognize it, an honest mistake that the police wouldn't be too concerned about rectifying, even if they thought there might be reason to do so.

Still, I probably should talk to the father.

"What was the father's name?" I asked. "Do you remember?"

"Not offhand. I can find out."

"Would you? I don't know if it's important or not, but I'd like to know, just in case."

"Shouldn't take too long to find out," he said. "I'll get back to you."

"Call as soon as you can," I said. I gave him my home phone number and the number at the skating rink.

"Right."

I called Jane Borman at her home.

"I'm just calling to remind you to bring the video-tape with you when you go to the rink today," I said.

"I'm just getting my things together right now. The tape is right beside me."

"Great," I said. "If I can't get you to go to dinner with me, at least we can have a tv date."

"I'm sorry, Leo. I'll set up the VCR for you, but you'll have to watch the tape by yourself. I'm going to be awfully busy getting ready for the show tonight."

"Oh."

"Come by about four o'clock. The show doesn't start until eight. That'll give you four hours, if you need that long."

Four hours in a bare room with an amateur video-tape. Who says private eyes don't endure hardship?

I had one more task, and I had to complete it before the sun set. At two o'clock I was in my car, driving slowly through Rock Creek Park, looking for the place where I had been ambushed two nights before.

It was a pleasant afternoon. The sun had crept out from behind its gray curtain, and the sunlight glinted on the snow banks.

I pulled into a parking lot above Pierce Mill and got out to look around. I walked along a hiking trail nearby that led past stands of pawpaw and maple, bare now in the snow. Through their uppermost branches I could see the gray roof of a squared-off building—the skating rink. I was beyond the mill now and above the zoo, in an area where only the most rigorous runners and cyclists came, even in the summertime. You could walk for days in Rock Creek Park and not exhaust the narrow winding trails and bike paths. Wildlife thrives in this improbable urban wilderness, too. I have seen opossum and rabbits and muskrats in the summer. There are supposed to be foxes and an occasional weasel, though I haven't seen them.

The path led deep into the woods to the edge of the creek. A thin layer of ice covered the surface of the creek, but I could see clear water running beneath it. I crossed the stream carefully on moss-covered stones. A solitary cardinal beat a hasty retreat from the limb of a nearby oak tree when he saw me coming. He alighted on another branch a few yards farther down the path.

There were mountains here once, distant cousins of the Blue Ridge of Virginia, but the years wore them down. Now these peaceful bluffs were all that remained.

The path followed the creek bed for a while, veered sharply away, then returned. I found a place where the ice layer had broken through. I poked my finger tentatively into the running water beneath. When I brought it up, it smelled faintly of creosote—probably runoff from a National Park Service fence-building project farther upstream.

Still farther along the path, the ridge was split by a steep, narrow ravine. I found there what I had been looking for—a series of rock outcroppings that formed a natural stairway to the top of the ridge.

I began to climb.

I came to a chain-link fence about halfway up the

ravine. The fence was old and badly rusted, but it was serviceable still. The Park Service had topped it with four strands of razor wire, which jutted in toward me at an angle. It would have been a formidable barrier except for the fact that someone had taken a pair of wire-cutting pliers and opened a passage about four feet high at the base of the fence. The cuts had been made recently, and the ends of the wire still gleamed, rust-free.

I slipped through the hole and continued climbing until I was close enough to the top of the ridge to see where I would come out. It was in a close wood, thick with dense, woody underbrush and tall pines. Beyond the pines I could see the square corner of a red-brick building. Parked outside was an ugly blue vehicle with enormous balloon tires. It was a Zamboni, the vehicle that shaved and resurfaced the ice at a skating rink.

I made my way back down the ravine and walked back to where I had parked my car. It seemed to take longer going back.

A light dusting of snow had fallen from the tree branches overhead onto the hood of my car. I brushed off the residue that had clung to my windshield and slipped into the driver's seat. I swung the car out on Beach Drive and headed north.

About a mile farther down, I reached another road that led upward, out of the park. I took it, and as I crept up the ridge I looked down and saw the other thing I had known I would find. Below me was the small parking area with the chain across the entrance and a turnaround area in front of the chain. Across the road from the chain, a high snowbank had been thrown up by a snowplow. The snowbank was indented, as if a car had run into it. A late-model, blue Pontiac Grand Prix, to be precise.

Chapter Fourteen

Jane was waiting for me in the lobby of the skating rink. She smiled when she saw me, and the crinkles reappeared at the corners of her eyes. It occurred to me that she was probably older than I was. It occurred to me, also, that I didn't care.

I took her hand and squeezed it, and mine was squeezed in return.

"How are you?"

"Very well, thank you," she said. "And you?"

"Fine."

"That's good. I'm glad."

"Thank you for asking."

"Oh, you're very welcome."

We were still holding hands, it seemed. I was eager to see the videotapes, but I didn't want to be the one to let go.

"You wanted to see some television," she said at last.

"Yes. Of course, I wanted to see it with you."

"Well, maybe I can stay for a little while, or come back now and then. I have students to teach, and the performers will be here shortly."

"Performers?"

"Remember the ice show? Irene told you about it. We're putting on a show in a couple of hours."

"I keep forgetting about it," I said. "I gather it's a big deal."

"If you're ten years old, and you've been practicing and taking lessons two or three times a week, your first appearance before an audience *is* a big deal. We've got lights, costumes, and music—the whole nine yards."

She led me to a lesson room at the rear of the building. We passed Jack Dumas's old office on the way. It was dark, and the door was shut.

The video recorder already had a tape loaded in its mouth. Jane closed the door behind us.

"I've already put in the tape and turned it on," she said. "Do you want it from the beginning?"

"Please."

She punched the PLAY button, and the screen of the small portable television turned silver-gray.

"It's just a black-and-white set," she said. "Will this do, or do you need color?"

"This is fine."

I could hear Jane's voice over the television speaker announcing the date and time of the recording, and then Debbie and Jerry came into focus at center ice.

"Will you really learn something from this?" Jane asked me over my shoulder.

"I think so. I hope so."

She lay her hand softly on my shoulder. Off screen another Jane—the prerecorded Jane—shouted instructions to the tiny figures on the ice, who nodded in response.

The couple took position. Jerry stood, and Debbie knelt beside him, her right hand in his left, her left hand on the ice to steady herself. There was a moment of silence, and then the music blared from the speaker.

They began to skate. I couldn't tell how well their skating fit the music because the sound reverberated off the walls and came back indistinctly.

I felt Jane's hand lift from my shoulder and felt, rather than heard, the door swinging shut behind her. I turned to look after her, but she was gone.

The skaters performed their routine, and the camera followed them doggedly around the ice. Occasionally, Debbie and Jerry would get ahead, and the camera would swing erratically around to catch up.

When I reached the point at which Debbie fell, I stopped the tape. In the frozen frame I could see her foot flying out of control and her head dipping perilously close to the ice at a crazy angle. The picture was blurred, but I thought I could see the first shocked recognition on Jerry's face that something was going wrong.

They were very close to where they had started their routine.

I watched the tape again until I had seen what I had come to see. Then I ran it back and replayed it from the beginning. I replayed the tape over and over again.

On about the fifth replay, a teenager with big round glasses poked her head through the door.

"Mr. McFarlin?"

"That's right."

"Ms. Borman said I could find you in here. You

have a phone call. You can take it out front at the desk."

I followed her back toward the lobby.

"Do you know who's calling?"

"No. He didn't give his name."

I took the call standing at the open door of the box office while the girl with the glasses fussed over an adding machine in the corner.

"This is McFarlin."

The voice on the line said, "This is Ray Martin."

"You mean Harry Liston, don't you?"

He chuckled. "Not anymore. Harry's dead. I'm Ray Martin this year."

"For how long?"

"As long as it's useful. After that, we'll see."

I waited without replying.

"Do you know why I'm calling?"

"Why don't you tell me?"

"You've been getting close. I want you off my back."

"Is that why you took target practice at me the other night? A more direct approach might have been more effective."

"I wasn't sure you recognized me," he said. "I was wearing that brown wig and the sheepskin jacket, and it was dark. You're pretty good."

"It wasn't my powers of observation that did it," I said. "When I thought about it later, I realized I'd left a phone message at the rink that told you exactly where to find me. I assume it was posted on a bulletin board in plain view."

He laughed, but there wasn't much humor in it. "You were very helpful."

I thought briefly of trying to trace the call, but there wasn't any point to it. I could hear traffic noise behind him. He was calling from a pay phone on the street somewhere, and he would be gone long before we could get to him. Besides, the police would want an explanation before they would authorize a phone trace, and I couldn't provide it.

"I think we ought to talk," I said.

"About what?"

"About what you're doing to your wife and daughter, for instance. Don't you think they deserve an explanation?"

"My *widow* doesn't deserve an explanation," he said. "But I suppose you do. All right. Let's meet."

"I'll be here all afternoon," I said. "I'm in a lesson room in the back."

"Oh, no. I'm not stupid. Not there. Meet me at Jack Dumas's place. You know where it is?"

"He seemed to have two different addresses."

"That place on Euclid Place was my house," Martin said. "I mean the other place. You know where it is?"

"Yes. It'll take me about an hour to get there."

"That's fine."

"There's something else you ought to know," I lied. "When you ambushed me on the parkway I wasn't carrying a gun. I am now."

"Leave it in the car," he said. "You won't need it. I just want to talk." He hung up.

I could have made the trip in half the time, but I wanted a few more minutes with the videotape. I went back to the lesson room and rewound the tape to the beginning one more time. This time I turned off the sound. It was distracting, and I didn't need it.

Silently the black and silver skaters took their position. Silently Debbie gave her right hand to Jerry and knelt slowly on the ice.

Silently she placed her left hand on the ice and looked up at her partner. Silently they waited for what seemed forever. Silently they began to skate.

And silently, at the moment they crossed their original starting point, Debbie fell.

When I had seen enough, I rewound the tape and took it with me. I had a little time on my hands, so I drove back to my office and left the cassette in my safe. Then I headed back through the Saturday traffic to the house where Jack Dumas had lived to keep a rendezvous with a two-time murderer.

The front door of Dumas's house was locked. Although it had been dark outside for some time, there were no lights on inside. I walked around to the side of the house and tried the kitchen door. It was locked too.

"McFarlin."

It was a hoarse whisper from the direction of the garage. I turned and realized that the overhead door was open.

"Down here."

I came down the steps and stood outside, peering into the blackness.

"Where's your car?" I asked.

"Down the street. The garage here is too cluttered."

"Did you bring the Toyota or the Grand Prix?"

"So you knew about the Toyota, too," he said. "I brought the Pontiac. I disposed of the Toyota a couple of days ago. They'll find it in a few days in a corner of the parking lot at Springfield Mall."

"Why dispose of it? Did it get dusty?"

"Just a precaution," he said. "I don't like to keep things too long. The kind of life I live, you don't want to get too attached to things. Property is like fingerprints; it can give you away."

"Is that what life is like, as a nonperson?"

"That's right. Did you come unarmed, like I asked?"

"Yes."

"Good."

His indistinct form materialized at the garage entrance, and there was a small-bore semi-automatic in his hand. I would have bet it was the gun that had killed Dumas.

"You just wanted to talk, remember."

"I lied," he said.

He gestured with the automatic. "Get in here or I'll shoot you where you stand."

"Out here in the open?"

He shrugged. "Quiet residential neighborhood. People watching television, minding their own business. I'd have to empty the magazine before anybody took notice."

I couldn't think of any cogent rebuttal to that. I eased past him into the garage. He motioned me over against the wall while he pulled down the overhead door with his other hand.

"Back up," he said.

There wasn't much room. I took a couple of steps backward and felt a sawhorse jabbing into the back of my thighs. There was a faint smell of axle grease in the air, and motor oil as well.

"I thought you wanted to talk."

"Lie down," he said. I could make out his form in the darkness, but I couldn't see his face.

"Fifteen years is a long time to keep it to yourself," I said.

He moved suddenly, and his foot caught me in the ribs. I found myself sitting heavily on the concrete floor. It hurt like the devil.

"Lie down or I'll kick you again."

I laid down and found my face in a patch of grease. I heard him moving above me, but it was too dark to make out what he was doing.

"Why do you want to kill your own daughter? It doesn't make sense."

He grabbed my wrists and began winding heavy cord around them, which meant that he had to put the gun down for a moment. I rolled hard against his legs and felt him stagger backward. I came up into a crouch, trying to make out his form in the darkness.

I hesitated too long. I sprang forward, but he caught me under the chin with his knee and sent me sprawling back onto the concrete. My eyes were beginning to adjust to the darkness, but it didn't seem to be doing me a lot of good. I staggered to my feet and was met by a flailing roundhouse right that clipped my jaw hard. My head snapped back like a rubber band.

I moved in again, but he stepped away, reached behind his back, and came up with the gun. I considered my options and discovered that they had all run out.

"I ought to shoot you now," he said.

"Why?"

"You and Dumas," he said, ignoring my question. "Poking your nose in other people's business."

If he was willing to talk, maybe he wouldn't shoot just yet. Keep him talking, at all costs.

"What did Dumas do to you?"

"He came to see me with that ridiculous picture," Liston said. "He recognized me in the photograph, and he came to see me at my house on Euclid Place. He said he wanted me to go away for six months. After that I could come back, he said. I laughed at him. He offered me money."

"What did you do then?"

"I told him to go away for six months, himself. In six months I'd be gone, I told him. I'd waited fifteen years, and I was tired of waiting. It was my turn. But he wouldn't wait. He had a gun. He tried to shoot me."

"But he didn't succeed."

He snorted. "Guns have safety catches, usually. He pulled the trigger, but he forgot to remove the safety. He didn't get another chance."

"Why couldn't you go away like Dumas asked?"

"I had something to do."

"What did you have to do?"

"It doesn't matter now," he said. He backed slowly away from me, across the narrow garage, to where a stack of six-foot lengths of lumber lay against the far wall. He bent over and laid the gun on the concrete floor.

It was the only chance I would get, I thought. I moved as fast as I could, meaning to catch him in the gut and drive him against the wall. He straightened up, and I saw surprise and shock on his face, but no panic. He lifted a length of lumber over his head and slammed it down hard.

The force of my rush knocked him off his feet but did not stop the two-by-four from descending.

Barlow was right, I remember thinking. *I've been acting like a fool and a dilettante.*

The two-by-four slammed down again, against the back of my head. I thought briefly about the pain exploding in my skull, and then I quit thinking at all.

Chapter Fifteen

It was hot, very hot, and I could hardly breathe, and a bright orange light was penetrating my head, forcing me awake.

I didn't want to be awake. I wanted to sleep forever, or if not forever, until the pain in my head subsided, and until I could breathe again, and the summer went away, and the cool snow returned, and flickering orange light quit burrowing into my brain.

Let me sleep.

Let me stop hurting.

Let me stop burning.

Don't make me wake up.

Don't tie me up.

Why am I tied, hands and feet? Why do I hurt so much? And why is it so hot and so bright?

Flames flickered in my mind, and near the flames lay an overturned gasoline can, slowly blackening in the heat. The flames came, and went, and came again, until eventually it dawned on me that they were real, and not imaginary.

The flames are real.

The fire is real.

And the pain.

190

The pain raged through my body. My brain, always sensible, was of two opinions about it. It insisted, on one hand, on the necessity of sleep, of rest, of time to repair the damage and alleviate the trauma. It insisted, on the other hand, on action—quick and decisive action.

The garage is on fire. You must escape. Quickly.
But the pain, the terrible pain.
But the fire, the terrible fire.

The fire won, barely. It was leaping now, licking seductively at the rafters overhead. The rafters were not yet burning, I saw, but it was only a matter of time—and not much time, at that.

I tried to stand. I succeeded only in toppling backward and cracking my head sickeningly on the concrete floor. The fall was like a fresh beating, and a wave of pain washed over me. My hands and feet, I realized stupidly, were bound tight.

The pain subsided eventually, and I tried to think. It wasn't easy.

The first priority, obviously, was to release my hands and feet. It would be difficult enough to get out of a burning garage with my hands and feet free. Trussed like a roasting chicken, it would be impossible.

The question was: how to get loose.

There was an aluminum stepladder leaning against the wall on the far side of the garage, away from the flames. It occurred to me that there might be a rough edge on the ladder, something sharp, on which I could saw away the rope around my wrist.

I began to roll across the concrete floor, over and

over, slowly toward the stepladder. The fire by now had spread across the side wall behind me, and flames were beginning to melt an old tire that had been lying in the corner. The white sidewall was turning black, and the tire was giving off a foul odor. It reminded me that I had to worry about smoke and fumes as well as heat.

Every movement of my body brought a fresh wave of nausea and a renewed throbbing in my head. My left shoulder felt as if it had been stabbed, though there were no signs of bleeding.

The stepladder was getting closer, but I was making slow progress. The garage couldn't have been more than fifteen feet across, but it seemed like Death Valley.

I reached the ladder eventually and struggled into a sitting position with my back to it. It took several attempts. I stretched my arms behind me and searched blindly for sharp edges on the underside of the nearest rung.

No luck.

I shifted position and tried a little higher.

My hands caught on a burr on the metal surface, and I had a glimmer of hope. It was short-lived. I squirmed around to get a better angle and felt the ladder slip away from me. I looked around in time to see it crash to the floor.

It had fallen behind some old lumber, which was stacked up near the wall. I would never be able to reach it unless my hands were free and then, of course, I wouldn't need it.

I glanced upward. The fire had spread to the roof,

and it was working its way across to the opposite side of the garage. My air would be gone long before I would have to worry about the fire. Then the roof would give way, and the fire would consume me as quickly as it was now consuming the wall.

By that time I wouldn't be feeling the fire, or anything else. I probably wouldn't even be identifiable. There wouldn't be rope burns on my corpse because hardly any flesh would be left. And there certainly wouldn't be any rope. The fire would destroy the rope.

The fire would destroy the rope.

Yes.

No.

I looked again at the far wall, burning furiously now, and decided that I wanted no part of it. It could conceivably free my hands and feet—that was certainly clear—but it would require me to roll back across the floor again to where the flames were raging.

Even if I could cover the distance, I would never be able to get close enough to the fire to do any good. The heat was too intense. I was already closer to that wall of flame than I had any desire to be.

But if I couldn't go to the fire, perhaps the fire could come to me. Not all of it. Just a little bit. A two-by-four's worth.

There was a two-by-four at the top of the stack, but the one-by-six beneath it looked more maneuverable. I worked it out of the stack. I managed to twist it around and shove one end of it into the flames.

It seemed forever before the plank finally caught fire. When it seemed to be burning well, I pulled it back across the floor to me and spread my hands—as well as I could—over the burning end. I couldn't see what I was doing, but the heat of the fire guided me reasonably well.

I felt the heat scorching my wrist and smelled my own flesh beginning to burn. The smell made me gag, but I fought down the nausea and left my hands over the fire.

The rope burned through surprisingly quickly, and my hands were free. I spun on my butt and used the same technique on the ropes binding my feet. It was easier now because I could see what I was doing.

Now that my feet were free the problem became how to get out of the garage. I picked up a two-by-four and employed it as a battering ram on the door. The door was wooden, and my makeshift ram made short work of it. When it was first breached I took a running start and hit with all the strength I could muster.

I burst out of the garage into air so cold it hurt my chest, but it was the best pain I had ever felt. My clothes were on fire, and hair as well. I plunged into a high snowbank and rolled around. I could hear the sizzle as the fires went out. I rubbed snow all over the burned places, just to make sure.

I stood up and began to run. A small crowd had gathered across the street at a respectful distance, and I could hear fire sirens in the distance. I didn't wait, and nobody tried to stop me.

Six sugarplum fairies swirled and twinkled. The smallest of the six, a chubby-legged blond with a red ribbon in her hair, waved a thin wand topped with a foil-wrapped star. She waved it in tiny circles in time with the music, which was, of course, by Tchaikovsky.

The fairies, who must have been about five years old, launched themselves into an arabesque formation and glided six-abreast across the ice. Their costumes were covered with silver spangles, which glittered in the spotlight. Applause rippled through the audience of adoring friends and relatives.

Somewhere nearby a woman said, "Aren't they cute?"

I scanned the audience, but I didn't see Liston anywhere. I was at one end of the grandstand, which had been pulled down from the wall during the couple of hours I had been gone. There were about five hundred people in the audience, I estimated. Jane had been right; it *was* a big deal.

I walked the length of the stands and scanned the audience again. I didn't see Ray Martin/Harry Liston anywhere.

Maybe he hadn't come. Maybe he got scared and left town. I considered the possibility and dismissed it. He had been planning his next move for a long time, and he had lured me out to Dumas's house in order to get me out of the way. That meant his plans were still on.

He would be here sooner or later. But so would I. And I had an advantage because he would not be expecting to see me. He thought I was dead.

"The Dance of the Sugarplum Fairies" ended in mid-measure. The lights went out, and the fairies skated quickly to the sidelines and a dark passageway to the makeshift dressing rooms. Debbie and Jerry were down that passage, isolated in their own room. I walked that way and met Jane in the hallway.

"What in the world happened to you?" she asked. "You look awful."

"It's nothing. Don't worry about it."

"But you're burned. You should get to a hospital."

"It's not too bad. I'll worry about it later. Right now, there are more important things to worry about."

"If you say so."

"Any trouble yet?"

"No, but Debbie and Jerry are supposed to skate in about fifteen minutes. Should I let them go ahead? Is it safe?"

"If I tell you it isn't safe, will you advise them not to skate?"

"Of course."

"It isn't safe. Tell them not to skate."

She sighed and turned toward the dressing room. "I said I'd tell them, but I don't think Irene will go along with it. She wants Debbie to perform."

"Look," I said. "Ray Martin is our man. I know he's here somewhere, but until I find him Debbie isn't safe. So keep her in the dressing room until I find him. Okay?"

"But—"

"No buts," I said. "No questions. Just do it, please. I promise to find him as soon as I can."

"But I know where he is," she said.

I had already started moving away from her. Now I stopped and looked back at her.

"You do?"

She nodded. "We're short-handed tonight, so I put

him to work on the Zamboni. He's supposed to resurface the ice just before Debbie and Jerry perform." A look of horror crossed her face. "You don't think he's going to drop something on the ice again?"

"No, I think his method will be a little more direct than that." I headed in the direction of the area where they parked the Zamboni.

"I'm sorry, Leo," she said. "I didn't know Ray was involved in this."

"I know. I didn't tell you. Just stay close to Debbie. Don't let her out of your sight until I get back."

The Zamboni was parked in a dark pit near the passageway that the fairies had taken. If I were to hang back in the darkness there I would be able to see him without being seen myself. I needed an element of surprise.

"Mr. McFarlin?"

It was the round-eyed teenager who worked in the box office. "There's a phone call for you. You can take it in my office again."

I shook my head. "Ask if I can call them back."

"He said it was urgent. I said I wasn't sure I could find you, and he said that I had to try—that it was vitally important."

I couldn't imagine what it could be, but I said, "all right," and followed her to the lobby.

It was Pete Blenheim on the phone.

"You wanted me to take another look at the Liston case," he said. "It took me a while, but I finally found somebody who worked on the case. He's retired now, but he remembers the name of Harry's father."

I sighed. "Pete, I'm sorry to do this to you after you

went to all that trouble, but the information just isn't urgent anymore."

"Well, you'll have to be the judge of that," he said. "Does that mean you've got the case wrapped up?"

"Just about."

"That's good. It sounded messy."

"It still is."

"Well, look, do you want me to just send you this information in the mail? Would that be better?"

"That's a good idea," I said. "I've got to get back to my post right now." Out on the ice the music ended, and the applause began. Next came the resurfacing, and then Debbie and Jerry would skate.

"Okay, I'll do it," he said. "This information probably isn't vital. It's a little unusual for a son to take his mother's name, but I don't suppose he cared much for his old man after he walked out on the family."

Something clicked deep inside me.

"What was that?"

"Harry's mother was named Liston, and he took his mother's name a year or two after his mother and father separated," Blenheim said.

"So his father's name wasn't Liston?"

"That's what I've been telling you."

I could hear the announcer calling for a short intermission. I could hear the stomping and shouting as five hundred kids and grownups began to climb down from the bleachers and pour into the lobby.

I could hear the Zamboni starting up.

"If Liston was his mother's name," I said, keeping my voice as even as I could, "what was his *father's* name?"

"I thought you wanted me to mail this to you."

"I just changed my mind again. What was his father's name?"

"It was Hollister," Blenheim said. "Full name Brewster Wellington Hollister. Quite a mouthful. Seems I've heard that name somewhere before."

My heart sank.

"There's something else interesting," he went on. "I don't know if it means anything, but I just noticed that Liston's body was identified exactly sixteen years ago today. Ironic, huh?"

"That's just great," I said.

"I guess the name means something to you, huh?"

"Yeah," I said. "It means I've been trying to protect the wrong person."

It was tough going, fighting the crowd as it poured out of the arena into the lobby. I managed to get inside in time to see Liston, riding the Zamboni, make a long sweep of the length of the ice, reach the end, and turn to make the long sweep again.

Hollister was sitting at the far end with Irene Liston at his side. He wore a camel-colored cashmere topcoat that he hadn't bothered to unbutton. He was listening intently as Irene chattered brightly beside him. He hadn't seen Liston and probably wouldn't have recognized him if he had.

But Harry recognized his father. As he reached Hollister's end of the ice, Liston reached quickly inside his jacket and withdrew the little gun he had pulled on me earlier in the evening.

All I could do was shout, so I shouted.

"Hollister! Get down!"

Hollister looked around, trying to locate the person who had called his name. Irene spoke to him, and he peered in my direction. This wasn't what I had in mind.

"Get down, Hollister!" He responded with a wave and a tentative smile. Was I an irate constituent? A political opponent? A lobbyist?

The Zamboni slowed for the turn. Liston stood in his seat, leaned casually over the glass barrier, and pumped two quick shots into Senator Brewster Wellington Hollister, Democrat of Missouri.

Hollister slumped. Irene put her hands to her face. A woman near me screamed. A man shouted. It might have been me.

Liston rapidly wheeled the Zamboni around in a three-quarter turn and disappeared back into the parking area. In a moment I felt a blast of cold air and heard the machine pass through the overhead doors to the outside.

I took a shortcut across the ice.

Chapter Sixteen

The footprints, of course, led into the woods.

Liston had left the Zamboni behind the rink with the engine still running and had pushed his way through a break in a hedgerow.

I pushed through the opening after him. The tracks changed to snowshoe prints. He must have had them stashed away in anticipation.

Below me, I knew, was the freshly opened slit in the chain-link fence. Below that was Rock Creek Park.

He would be hard to trace in the park. He could head down the hill to the trickling creek, move upstream along the creek bed for a mile or so, and come out of the woods on the other side. The thin ice cover would break under him, and his feet would be wet when he came out, but no doubt he had a change of socks and shoes in his car.

There would be a car parked down there, and I had a pretty good idea where it would be. Harry and I had been there before.

And I still had my advantage. He may have heard me warning Hollister, but he couldn't have known who it was. Sound distorted badly inside the skating rink.

So he still thought I was dead.

I ran for my car. At least I could beat him to his ultimate destination. I could drive faster than he could travel on snowshoes.

"Mr. McFarlin!"

Irene Liston was clopping toward me in her high heels.

"You know that the Senator has been killed!"

"Yes, I saw it."

She searched my face carefully, as if looking for me to confirm what she already knew.

"Did you recognize the man who shot him?"

"He worked here under the name of Ray Martin," I said. "You and I both know his real name."

"Oh, no," she said softly. "The moment I saw him I was afraid it was Harry. I never really believed he was dead. But he must have worked the day shift here; I never saw him around."

"I don't think he wanted you to see him. I think he made a point of remaining out of sight when you were here."

I opened the door to my car and slipped behind the wheel. Irene hurried around and got in on the passenger side.

I shook my head. "Stay here and call the police. That's more helpful."

"It's already been done."

"All right," I said. "But stay in the car. Don't let him see you. He's skittish enough as it is. Remember he's got a gun, and you're not his favorite person."

There was fresh snow falling again, with sleet in it. I drove carefully down the narrow road into the park.

The snow that blew across the windshield had a mes-
merizing effect, and it had been a long day. I hurt a
lot and needed a rest.

There was a BMW parked in the turnaround this
time. Harry had obviously anticipated some high-
speed driving and had stolen his getaway car accord-
ingly.

Liston wasn't there yet. I had beaten him to the
parking area, assuming that I had guessed right about
his intentions.

I parked precariously on the roadside a little distance away, halfway up the hill where he couldn't see
my car. I walked the rest of the way back in.

The gun was the thing to worry about. It wasn't
much of a gun, and he certainly wasn't much of an
expert with it. Still, it had already killed two people.
A gun is a gun.

Next the car. That was a simpler challenge. I had a
pocketknife, and a few minutes later the BMW had
two flat tires.

In desperation I took up position behind a tree and
began making snowballs. I found small stones on the
ground and packed them into the centers. Then I
packed the snow hard and tight around them and took
the finished products down to the creek. There I broke
the thin layer of ice and dipped the snowballs in the
running water. The snowballs froze almost immediately.

I borrowed a floor mat from the BMW and laid it
on the ground. I stacked the snowballs on it to keep
them from freezing to the ground.

He came out of the woods about ten minutes later,

fifty yards away, still wearing the snowshoes. At the edge of the clearing he shed the snowshoes and began to run. The gun must have been in his pocket.

I let him get past. When he was about twenty feet beyond me, I fired the first snowball. It missed and crashed behind him in the woods. The sound brought him up short, and he turned in the direction of the noise. He reached for his gun.

The second snowball caught him square on the cheek. He turned in my direction, fumbling with the safety catch on the gun. The third snowball caught him in the Adam's apple. He dropped the gun, and both hands went to his throat.

When he realized what he had done, he dropped to the ground to search for the gun. I reached him about the time he got to it. I landed hard on his back, hoping to bring him to the ground.

It just made him angry. He reared and tried to throw me off, but I gripped him around the neck, and we both went sprawling in the snow. The gun clattered away.

He went for the gun again, but I caught him at the knees and sent him sprawling once more. He rolled onto his back and got one knee up to push me away.

I got my knee in first and caught him in the chest, but it didn't faze Liston. He threw a hard roundhouse right that would have dislocated my jaw if it had connected. I slipped inside and caught it on my back, instead. It still hurt.

He was trying to reach the gun with his right hand, so I pinned his arms. Immediately his knees came up again and flipped me in midair. He was on me before I knew what had happened.

He was about my height, but he was probably twenty pounds heavier, and the weight began to win out. I struggled, but I was pinned with his legs. His hands went around my throat. I couldn't get any leverage.

I could feel myself weakening, slipping away. The pressure was spreading to my chest, and the world was growing dark. I could barely see, or think. The end seemed near.

The end, in fact, *was* near, but it wasn't the end I had been expecting.

Suddenly the pressure and pain were gone. The light came gradually back, and I could feel the snow beneath me, cold and wet.

Harry Liston was gone.

I struggled to a sitting position. Liston lay beside me, face up, eyes open, pupils fixed and dilated. There was a bullet hole in his temple.

Irene Liston stood over him with the gun in her hand.

"Thank you," I said.

"You're welcome."

I stood up and tried walking around. I was a bit unsteady but otherwise okay.

She looked down at the corpse, which stared blindly back at her.

"Poor Harry," she said. "You were never half the man your father was. Dead or alive." Flinching a bit, she pulled the trigger again. The body on the ground jerked from the impact.

I fought back a wave of nausea.

"Mrs. Liston, he was already dead," I said.

She shook her head sadly. "He shot his father twice," she said.

On Monday I had a martini.

It came in a slender, long-stemmed glass that opened into a wide-mouthed bell at the top, like a flattened tulip. It was a nearly perfect martini glass, and the liquid inside wasn't bad, either. Even the solitary olive at the bottom was good when I finally drank my way down to it, though I found myself wondering who had beat me to the pimento.

The chair in which I sat was the perfect martini-drinker's chair: low-slung, high-backed with high armrests, covered in some breathable vinyl facsimile of leather. Streamlined but comfortably so, like an Art Deco movie house. The martini is, after all, an Art Deco sort of drink.

The bandages bothered me a little, and my hair still smelled of smoke and scorched flesh, but it was a minor irritation.

The perfect drink, in the perfect chair, which was situated in the perfect place: a lawyer's office on Connecticut Avenue. My host—and bartender—was Jim Hilliard, the lawyer who had designs on my sister.

"You're feeling better, I trust?" Hilliard asked, favoring me with his concerned expression. "No lasting effects from your adventurous evening?"

"I got some burns, but they're healing," I said. "The hospital treated me as an outpatient, so I guess they weren't too concerned."

"I suppose," said Hilliard, "that I should have taken you more seriously."

"I beg your pardon?"

"I said I should have taken you more seriously. When we met, you said you might have occasion to steer a little business my way. I didn't pay a lot of attention at the time."

"You never know where your next buck is coming from," I said, and sipped my martini. It came out sounding smug, which was the way I meant it.

"Well, you've certainly brought me a client," he said. "And a well-paying client, at that. Lawyers aren't supposed to talk about money—we're supposed to be above all that—but I don't mind telling you that I like money and the people who have it."

"She doesn't have it yet," I pointed out. "It's true that Hollister's will leaves her virtually everything, but long-lost relatives are virtually coming out of the woodwork."

"Doesn't matter," Hilliard said. "She's got me representing her. She'll get it." He took a long sip from his own martini, and I marveled again at his enthusiasm.

"She'll have to do some time in prison," I said.

"For murdering Harry Liston? For murdering a murderer and saving your life? It'll be a light sentence, at most. I might even be able to get her a commendation of some sort."

He frowned. "I wish she hadn't shot Liston twice, though. Without that second shot, I might have been able to make some sort of self-defense plea."

"Tough break."

"Why did she do that, do you suppose? Why'd she shoot him again after he was dead?"

I shrugged. "Some people like to keep score," I said.

He rose and strolled to the credenza where he had set up the martini pitcher. I'd never seen anyone who actually mixed martinis from scratch, before. Well, maybe in a James Bond movie.

"How about another?"

"No, thanks. I've got work to do this afternoon, and I'm on antibiotics."

He turned back to the bar and began mixing another for himself.

"I don't care about the will," he said. "The will isn't essential; it's just gravy. There's going to be a book out of this, and a film, too, if we play our cards right. The whole affair is so complicated, and sordid, and banal that it can't help but be a best seller, if I can find the right ghostwriter."

"Washington's full of ghostwriters," I said.

"It can't be just anybody," he said. "I want someone who'll tell Irene's story sympathetically, with the right balance of pathos and bathos." He cocked an eye at me. "Interested?"

"I was a reporter, not a writer. No, thanks."

He shrugged. "We'll find somebody. As you say, Washington is full of ghostwriters."

I drained the martini and set the glass gently on a glass cocktail table. Out the window I could see pigeons strutting on the sidewalk in Farragut Square. It was a warm day for December, and even the homeless street people were enjoying the sunshine. Life was full.

"Why do you suppose Hollister identified a corpse as his son?" Hilliard asked me. "He must have known it wasn't Harry."

"I expect he knew. I don't know why he made the identification, though." "Why do you *think* he did it?"

"I think Harry had become a nuisance to him, and Hollister didn't want this liability popping up in his life after he returned to Missouri. He probably had Congressional aspirations even then."

"So why didn't Harry walk into a police station and say, 'Hey, look, I'm alive?' "

"Because Harry Liston was a wanted man. If he walked into a police station, they would have arrested him and charged him with two murders."

"So instead he just went to the hall of records in Rochester and obtained a spare identity," Hilliard said.

"My guess is he obtained several," I said. "I think Harry was a little repertory company, all by himself."

"I'd have thought Hollister did Harry a favor," Hilliard said. "I mean, having him declared dead, and all. Why would Harry want to kill him?"

"I don't know," I said. "It can't be pleasant knowing that your own father wanted you to be dead, and that's what Hollister was saying, essentially."

"So it was an ego thing? In that case, why did he wait so long? Why not do it right away?"

"In the beginning, he was probably too busy running to think about it much," I said. "I expect the resentment built up over the years. As the years went by, and he had to worry less about being caught, he got angrier and angrier. And yesterday was the sixteenth anniversary of the outrage."

Hilliard thought about this.

"Your basic garden-variety sociopath," he said finally.

"Maybe," I said. "At any rate, he certainly had a strong sense of outrage about injustices to Harry Liston."

I stood to go, and Hilliard came around from behind his desk to show me to the door. I had the feeling he didn't do that very often.

"I'll probably be calling you to testify, you know."

"I know."

"If you see Susan this evening, please apologize to her on my behalf," he said. "We were going out tonight, but things have come up."

"Having dinner with your client?"

"Why, yes, as a matter of fact. All part of the job."

"I'll extend your apologies."

I stepped into the hallway and headed for the reception area.

"By the way," Hilliard said. He tried to make it sound casual, like an afterthought. "Who was making all those threats on Irene's daughter if it wasn't her husband? Did you ever figure that out?"

I thought about what I had seen on the videotape and about the inevitable conclusion.

"Nope," I said. "Never did."

I found her at the skating rink staring out through the barricade at the ice. It was the lull between public skating sessions, and the Zamboni was at work resurfacing the ice. Debbie stood alone on the sidelines, with neither friends nor coaches in attendance. For the

first time since I had met her, she looked like the adolescent she was.

She glanced at me as I approached, then looked list-
lessly away. I stood behind her for a moment, then
moved so that I was standing beside her.

"You know I'll have to testify," I said.

I could see the throbbing in her carotid artery. The
Zamboni made a sweep of the ice.

"They'll probably ask me about those threats on
your life. Your mother's lawyer asked me about it just
an hour ago."

She shivered, just slightly.

"If they asked me today, I could honestly say that
I don't know who was behind them. But you should
know that I spent quite a lot of time the other day
watching the videotape of your fall, and I've been
thinking a lot about who could have tampered with
your skates."

"What did you decide?" she said.

"It seemed to me that only one person was in a
position both to sabotage your skates and leave that
paper clip where you would be sure to trip on it. And
it wasn't Jack Dumas."

She started to speak, but I put a finger to her lips
before she could do so.

"I'm aware that you haven't been happy as a competitive skater," I said. "I'm also aware that Philip
would do just about anything you asked. He clearly
made those threatening calls at somebody's instiga-
tion, but he couldn't have tampered with your skates
without being recognized. So I have a pretty good idea
what happened."

"If you know," she said, "why don't you tell?"

"I said I have a pretty good idea. I don't *know* in any way that a court would care about, and right now I prefer to leave it that way."

"Why?"

"Do you want to stop skating?"

"I did," she said. "Before."

"And now?"

She stared silently at the ice. A tear had formed in the corner of her eye, and she brushed it away with her finger.

"Did you know they've started a fund-raising drive for me?" she said, finally.

"No, I didn't."

"Jane told me about it this morning. They've sent announcements to all the radio and television stations. There was a television news crew here this morning interviewing Jane. It's all to help me keep skating while the trial goes on."

She turned to look at me. The tear had been replaced by others.

"Before, I did it to please my mother," she said. "Now, it's everybody. If I quit, I'm letting down all those people who contribute to the fund. And Jane, too. I've got responsibilities."

"What about your own needs?"

"I thought about my own needs once," she said. "Look how it turned out."

The Zamboni had finished its sweep of the ice. The surface glistened, and wisps of steam rose in the air.

"I love skating," she said. "I don't like competing.

But I couldn't afford to come here and pay my way. If I don't compete, I don't skate."

The Zamboni trundled slowly toward the opposite end of the rink and stopped. The driver hopped down and made his way gingerly toward the barrier. He pushed apart two sections, returned to the Zamboni and drove off the ice.

"Besides," she said, "I owe it to my mother. If I stopped now, after all she's done for me, it would kill her."

"Your mother killed your father. She didn't do that for you."

"She's still my mother."

The Zamboni had left the ice only seconds before, but the ice was already hardening, covering the etch marks of a hundred skate blades. Amazing how quickly you could erase the past, if you had the proper tools. Wellington Hollister, the late senator from Missouri, had understood all about that. So had his son.

"All right," I said. "If they ask me at the trial, I'll say I don't know who made those threats against you."

"Thank you."

"It may not come up, anyway. The judge may consider it irrelevant, although your mother's lawyer will certainly try to get it in the record."

I left her there. When I turned back from the doorway, she was still standing in the same place, a short, pretty, surprisingly frail girl in a green dress, who would probably be a champion someday in spite of herself.

I looked for Jane, but I didn't see her. It was just as well. I had business with my sister.

I drove down Connecticut Avenue some distance toward downtown until the evening rush hour became pretty heavy. I pulled off into a service station for gas. After I had filled my tank, I pulled to the edge of the apron and called Susan from a public phone. She wasn't at the television station—it was her day off, apparently—so I called her at home.

"This is your brother," I said, "and I have an idea."

"This I have to hear."

"Here it is: if you will spring for dinner—since you are more affluent than I—I will, in turn, spring for an evening of Gershwin, Jerome Kern, and Harold Arlen at the St. Regis Hotel."

"Who," she said, "is Harold Arlen?"

"You'll love him. He wrote 'The Man That Got Away.' How about it?"

"Does that mean you'll go with me to Phoenix for Christmas?"

"I'll think about it."

She sighed. "I suppose that will have to do," she said. "I'll pick you up at eight."

"Why don't I pick you up?" I said.

"No, thanks," she said. "I've ridden in your car before. Be waiting out front when I get there; I'm not coming up to get you."

We hung up, and I drove home. I took a long nap, and a long shower, and I spent a long time thinking. I thought about what Susan had said about my responsibilities, and I thought about Debbie Liston and her responsibilities, and about the mother to whom she remained loyal, in spite of everything.

By choosing not to tell everything I knew at the

trial, I was in a way feeding her sense of guilt and shame. A psychiatrist would probably call me a co-dependent. The thing was, I still thought it was the right choice. Maybe the world needed a few more co-dependents.

When I had finished thinking, I called the airlines. It took a bit of searching because it was the holiday season and the planes were pretty full, but I finally managed to finagle a round-trip ticket to Phoenix.

What's that old saying? "Home is where, when you go there, they have to take you in."

I guessed it was time to put it to the test.